ANGELA CARTER

THE BLOODY CHAMBER
AND OTHER STORIES

PENGUIN BOOKS

PENGUIN BOOKS

Published by the Penguin Group
Penguin Books Ltd, 27 Wrights Lane, London W8 5TZ, England
Penguin Books USA Inc., 375 Hudson Street, New York, New York 10014, USA
Penguin Books Australia Ltd, Ringwood, Victoria, Australia
Penguin Books Canada Ltd, 10 Alcorn Avenue, Toronto, Ontario, Canada M4V 3B2
Penguin Books (NZ) Ltd, 182–190 Wairau Road, Auckland 10, New Zealand

Penguin Books Ltd, Registered Offices: Harmondsworth, Middlesex, England

First published by Victor Gollancz Ltd 1979
First published in the United States of America by Harper & Row, Publishers, Inc., 1981
Published in Penguin Books 1981
17 19 20 18 16

Some of the stories in this collection originally appeared, in
somewhat different form, in the following publications: 'The
Courtship of My Lyon', British *Vogue*; 'The Erl-King' and 'The
Company of Wolves', *Bananas*; 'The Lady of the House of Love',
The Iowa Review; 'The Werewolf', *South-West Arts Review*;
'Wolf-Alice', *Stand*. All are reprinted here with the permission of
the editors. 'The Snow Child' was broadcast on the BBC Radio 4
programme *Not Now, I'm Listening*. 'Puss-in-Boots' appeared in an
anthology, *The Straw and the Gold*, edited by Emma
Tennant (Pierrot Books, 1979).

Printed in England by Clays Ltd, St Ives plc
Set in Monotype Ehrhart

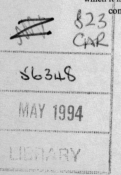

Contents

The Bloody Chamber

I remember how, that night, I lay awake in the wagon-lit in a tender, delicious ecstasy of excitement, my burning cheek pressed against the impeccable linen of the pillow and the pounding of my heart mimicking that of the great pistons ceaselessly thrusting the train that bore me through the night, away from Paris, away from girlhood, away from the white, enclosed quietude of my mother's apartment, into the unguessable country of marriage.

And I remember I tenderly imagined how, at this very moment, my mother would be moving slowly about the narrow bedroom I had left behind for ever, folding up and putting away all my little relics, the tumbled garments I would not need any more, the scores for which there had been no room in my trunks, the concert programmes I'd abandoned; she would linger over this torn ribbon and that faded photograph with all the half-joyous, half-sorrowful emotions of a woman on her daughter's wedding day. And, in the midst of my bridal triumph, I felt a pang of loss as if, when he put the gold band on my finger, I had, in some way, ceased to be her child in becoming his wife.

Are you sure, she'd said when they delivered the gigantic box that held the wedding dress he'd bought me, wrapped up in tissue paper and red ribbon like a Christmas gift of crystallized fruit. Are you sure you love him? There was a dress for her, too; black silk, with the dull, prismatic sheen of oil on water, finer than anything she'd worn since that adventurous girlhood in Indo-China, daughter of a rich tea planter. My eagle-featured, indomitable mother; what other student at the Conservatoire could boast that her mother had outfaced a junkful of Chinese pirates, nursed a village through a visitation of the plague, shot a man-eating tiger with her own hand and all before she was as old as I?

'Are you sure you love him?'

'I'm sure I want to marry him,' I said.

And would say no more. She sighed, as if it was with reluctance that she might at last banish the spectre of poverty from its habitual place at our meagre table. For my mother herself had gladly, scandalously, defiantly beggared herself for love; and, one fine day, her gallant soldier never returned from the wars, leaving his wife and child a legacy of tears that never quite dried, a cigar box full of medals and the antique service revolver that my mother, grown magnificently eccentric in hardship, kept always in her reticule, in case – how I teased her – she was surprised by footpads on her way home from the grocer's shop.

Now and then a starburst of lights spattered the drawn blinds as if the railway company had lit up all the stations through which we passed in celebration of the bride. My satin nightdress had just been shaken from its wrappings; it had slipped over my young girl's pointed breasts and shoulders, supple as a garment of heavy water, and now teasingly caressed me, egregious, insinuating, nudging between my thighs as I shifted restlessly in my narrow berth. His kiss, his kiss with tongue and teeth in it and a rasp of beard, had hinted to me, though with the same exquisite tact as this nightdress he'd given me, of the wedding night, which would be voluptuously deferred until we lay in his great ancestral bed in the sea-girt, pinnacled domain that lay, still, beyond the grasp of my imagination ... that magic place, the fairy castle whose walls were made of foam, that legendary habitation in which he had been born. To which, one day, I might bear an heir. Our destination, my destiny.

Above the syncopated roar of the train, I could hear his even, steady breathing. Only the communicating door kept me from my husband and it stood open. If I rose up on my elbow, I could see the dark, leonine shape of his head and my nostrils caught a whiff of the opulent male scent of leather and spices that always accompanied him and sometimes, during his courtship, had been the only hint he gave me that he had come into my mother's sitting room, for, though he was a big man, he moved as softly as if all his shoes had soles of velvet, as if his footfall turned the carpet into snow.

He had loved to surprise me in my abstracted solitude at the piano. He would tell them not to announce him, then soundlessly open the door and softly creep up behind me with his bouquet of hot-house flowers or his box of marrons glacés, lay his offering upon the keys and clasp his hands over my eyes as I was lost in a Debussy prelude. But that perfume of spiced leather always betrayed him; after my first shock, I was forced always to mimic surprise, so that he would not be disappointed.

He was older than I. He was much older than I; there were streaks of pure silver in his dark mane. But his strange, heavy, almost waxen face was not lined by experience. Rather, experience seemed to have washed it perfectly smooth, like a stone on a beach whose fissures have been eroded by successive tides. And sometimes that face, in stillness when he listened to me playing, with the heavy eyelids folded over eyes that always disturbed me by their absolute absence of light, seemed to me like a mask, as if his real face, the face that truly reflected all the life he had led in the world before he met me, before, even, I was born, as though that face lay underneath this mask. Or else, elsewhere. As though he had laid by the face in which he had lived for so long in order to offer my youth a face unsigned by the years.

And, elsewhere, I might see him plain. Elsewhere. But, where?

In, perhaps, that castle to which the train now took us, that marvellous castle in which he had been born.

Even when he asked me to marry him, and I said: 'Yes,' still he did not lose that heavy, fleshy composure of his. I know it must seem a curious analogy, a man with a flower, but sometimes he seemed to me like a lily. Yes. A lily. Possessed of that strange, ominous calm of a sentient vegetable, like one of those cobra-headed, funereal lilies whose white sheaths are curled out of a flesh as thick and tensely yielding to the touch as vellum. When I said that I would marry him, not one muscle in his face stirred, but he let out a long, extinguished sigh. I thought: Oh! how he must want me! And it was as though the imponderable weight of his desire was a force I might not withstand, not by virtue of its violence but because of its very gravity.

He had the ring ready in a leather box lined with crimson velvet, a fire opal the size of a pigeon's egg set in a complicated circle of dark antique gold. My old nurse, who still lived with my mother and me, squinted at the ring askance: opals are bad luck, she said. But this opal had been his own mother's ring, and his grandmother's, and her mother's before that, given to an ancestor by Catherine de Medici ... every bride that came to the castle wore it, time out of mind. And did he give it to his other wives and have it back from them? asked the old woman rudely; yet she was a snob. She hid her incredulous joy at my marital coup – her little Marquise – behind a façade of fault-finding. But, here, she touched me. I shrugged and turned my back pettishly on her. I did not want to remember how he had loved other women before me, but the knowledge often teased me in the threadbare self-confidence of the small hours.

I was seventeen and knew nothing of the world; my Marquis had been married before, more than once, and I remained a little bemused that, after those others, he should now have chosen me. Indeed, was he not still in mourning for his last wife? Tsk, tsk, went my old nurse.

And even my mother had been reluctant to see her girl whisked off by a man so recently bereaved. A Romanian countess, a lady of high fashion. Dead just three short months before I met him, a boating accident, at his home, in Brittany. They never found her body but I rummaged through the back copies of the society magazines my old nanny kept in a trunk under her bed and tracked down her photograph. The sharp muzzle of a pretty, witty, naughty monkey; such potent and bizarre charm, of a dark, bright, wild yet worldly thing whose natural habitat must have been some luxurious interior decorator's jungle filled with potted palms and tame, squawking parakeets.

Before that? *Her* face is common property; everyone painted her but the Redon engraving I liked best, *The Evening Star Walking on the Rim of Night.* To see her skeletal, enigmatic grace, you would never think she had been a barmaid in a café in Montmartre until Puvis de Chavannes saw her and had her expose her flat breasts and elongated thighs to his brush. And yet it was the absinthe doomed her, or so they said.

The first of all his ladies? That sumptuous diva; I had heard her sing Isolde, precociously musical child that I was, taken to the opera for a birthday treat. My first opera; I had heard her sing Isolde. With what white-hot passion had she burned from the stage! So that you could tell she would die young. We sat high up, halfway to heaven in the gods, yet she half-blinded me. And my father, still alive (oh, so long ago), took hold of my sticky little hand, to comfort me, in the last act, yet all I heard was the glory of her voice.

Married three times within my own brief lifetime to three different graces, now, as if to demonstrate the eclecticism of his taste, he had invited me to join this gallery of beautiful women, I, the poor widow's child with my mouse-coloured hair that still bore the kinks of the plaits from which it had so recently been freed, my bony hips, my nervous, pianist's fingers.

He was rich as Croesus. The night before our wedding – a simple affair, at the Mairie, because his countess was so recently gone – he took my mother and me, curious coincidence, to see *Tristan.* And, do you know, my heart swelled and ached so during the Liebestod that I thought I must truly love him. Yes. I did. On his arm, all eyes were upon me. The whispering crowd in the foyer parted like the Red Sea to let us through. My skin crisped at his touch.

How my circumstances had changed since the first time I heard those voluptuous chords that carry such a charge of deathly passion in them! Now, we sat in a loge, in red velvet armchairs, and a braided, bewigged flunkey brought us a silver bucket of iced champagne in the interval. The froth spilled over the rim of my glass and drenched my hands, I thought: My cup runneth over. And I had on a Poiret dress. He had prevailed upon my reluctant mother to let him buy my trousseau; what would I have gone to him in, otherwise? Twice-darned underwear, faded gingham, serge skirts, hand-me-downs. So, for the opera, I wore a sinuous shift of white muslin tied with a silk string under the breasts. And everyone stared at me. And at his wedding gift.

His wedding gift, clasped round my throat. A choker of rubies, two inches wide, like an extraordinarily precious slit throat.

After the Terror, in the early days of the Directory, the aristos who'd escaped the guillotine had an ironic fad of tying a red ribbon round their necks at just the point where the blade would have sliced it through, a red ribbon like the memory of a wound. And his grand-mother, taken with the notion, had her ribbon made up in rubies; such a gesture of luxurious defiance! That night at the opera comes back to me even now ... the white dress; the frail child within it; and the flashing crimson jewels round her throat, bright as arterial blood.

I saw him watching me in the gilded mirrors with the assessing eye of a connoisseur inspecting horseflesh, or even of a housewife in the market, inspecting cuts on the slab. I'd never seen, or else had never acknowledged, that regard of his before, the sheer carnal avarice of it; and it was strangely magnified by the monocle lodged in his left eye. When I saw him look at me with lust, I dropped my eyes but, in glancing away from him, I caught sight of myself in the mirror. And I saw myself, suddenly, as he saw me, my pale face, the way the muscles in my neck stuck out like thin wire. I saw how much that cruel necklace became me. And, for the first time in my innocent and confined life, I sensed in myself a potentiality for corruption that took my breath away.

The next day, we were married.

The train slowed, shuddered to a halt. Lights; clank of metal; a voice declaring the name of an unknown, never-to-be visited station; silence of the night; the rhythm of his breathing, that I should sleep with, now, for the rest of my life. And I could not sleep. I stealthily sat up, raised the blind a little and huddled against the cold window that misted over with the warmth of my breathing, gazing out at the dark platform towards those rectangles of domestic lamplight that promised warmth, company, a supper of sausages hissing in a pan on the stove for the station master, his children tucked up in bed asleep in the brick house with the painted shutters . . . all the paraphernalia of the every-day world from which I, with my stunning marriage, had exiled myself.

Into marriage, into exile; I sensed it, I knew it – that, henceforth, I would always be lonely. Yet that was part of the already familiar weight of the fire opal that glimmered like a gypsy's magic ball, so that I could not take my eyes off it when I played the piano. This ring, the bloody bandage of rubies, the wardrobe of clothes from Poiret and Worth, his scent of Russian leather – all had conspired to seduce me so utterly that I could not say I felt one single twinge of regret for the world of tartines and maman that now receded from me as if drawn away on a string, like a child's toy, as the train began to throb again as if in delighted anticipation of the distance it would take me.

The first grey streamers of the dawn now flew in the sky and an eldritch half-light seeped into the railway carriage. I heard no change in his breathing but my heightened, excited senses told me he was awake and gazing at me. A huge man, an enormous man, and his eyes, dark and motionless as those eyes the ancient Egyptians painted upon their sarcophagi, fixed upon me. I felt a certain tension in the pit of my stomach, to be so watched, in such silence. A match struck. He was igniting a Romeo y Julieta fat as a baby's arm.

'Soon,' he said in his resonant voice that was like the tolling of a bell and I felt, all at once, a sharp premonition of dread that lasted only as long as the match flared and I could see his white, broad face as if it were hovering, disembodied, above the sheets, illuminated from below like a grotesque carnival head. Then the flame died, the cigar glowed and filled the compartment with a remembered fragrance that made me think of my father, how he would hug me in a warm fug of Havana, when I was a little girl, before he kissed me and left me and died.

As soon as my husband handed me down from the high step of the train, I smelled the amniotic salinity of the ocean. It was November; the trees, stunted by the Atlantic gales, were bare and the lonely halt was deserted but for his leather-gaitered chauffeur waiting meekly beside the sleek black motor car. It was cold; I drew my furs about me, a wrap of white and black, broad stripes of ermine and sable, with a collar from which my head rose like the calyx of a wildflower. (I swear to you, I had never been vain until I met him.) The bell clanged; the straining train leapt its leash and left us at that lonely wayside halt where only he and I had descended. Oh, the wonder of it; how all that might of iron and steam had paused only to suit his convenience. The richest man in France.

'Madame.'

The chauffeur eyed me; was he comparing me, invidiously, to the countess, the artist's model, the opera singer? I hid behind my furs as if they were a system of soft shields. My husband liked me to wear my opal over my kid glove, a showy, theatrical trick – but the moment the ironic chauffeur glimpsed its simmering flash he smiled, as though it was proof positive I was his master's wife. And we drove towards the widening dawn, that now streaked half the sky with a wintry bouquet of pink of roses, orange of tiger-lilies, as if my husband had ordered me a sky from a florist. The day broke around me like a cool dream.

Sea; sand; a sky that melts into the sea – a landscape of misty pastels with a look about it of being continuously on the point of melting. A landscape with all the deliquescent harmonies of Debussy, of the études I played for him, the reverie I'd been playing that afternoon in the salon of the princess where I'd first met him, among the teacups and the little cakes, I, the orphan, hired out of charity to give them their digestive of music.

And, ah! his castle. The faery solitude of the place; with its turrets of misty blue, its courtyard, its spiked gate, his castle that lay on the very bosom of the sea with seabirds mewing about its attics, the casements opening on to the green and purple, evanescent departures of the ocean, cut off by the tide from land for half a day ... that castle, at home neither on the land nor on the water, a mysterious, amphibious place, contravening the materiality of both earth and the waves, with the melancholy of a mermaiden who perches on her rock and waits, endlessly, for a lover who had drowned far away, long ago. That lovely, sad, sea-siren of a place!

The tide was low; at this hour, so early in the morning, the causeway rose up out of the sea. As the car turned on to the wet cobbles between the slow margins of water, he reached out for my hand that had his sultry, witchy ring on it, pressed my fingers, kissed my palm with extraordinary tenderness. His face was as still as ever I'd seen it, still as a pond iced thickly over, yet his lips, that always looked so strangely red and naked between the black fringes of his beard, now curved a little. He smiled; he welcomed his bride home.

No room, no corridor that did not rustle with the sound of the sea and all the ceilings, the walls on which his ancestors in the stern regalia of rank lined up with their dark eyes and white faces, were stippled with refracted light from the waves which were always in motion; that luminous, murmurous castle of which I was the châtelaine, I, the little music student whose mother had sold all her jewellery, even her wedding ring, to pay the fees at the Conservatoire.

First of all, there was the small ordeal of my initial interview with the housekeeper, who kept this extraordinary machine, this anchored, castellated ocean liner, in smooth running order no matter who stood on the bridge; how tenuous, I thought, might be my authority here! She had a bland, pale, impassive, dislikeable face beneath the impeccably starched white linen head-dress of the region. Her greeting, correct but lifeless, chilled me; daydreaming, I dared presume too much on my status . . . briefly wondered how I might install my old nurse, so much loved, however cosily incompetent, in her place. Ill-considered schemings! He told me this one had been his foster mother; was bound to his family in the utmost feudal complicity, 'as much part of the house as I am, my dear'. Now her thin lips offered me a proud little smile. She would be my ally as long as I was his. And with that, I must be content.

But, here, it would be easy to be content. In the turret suite he had given me for my very own, I could gaze out over the tumultuous Atlantic and imagine myself the Queen of the Sea. There was a Bechstein for me in the music room and, on the wall, another wedding present – an early Flemish primitive of Saint Cecilia at her celestial organ. In the prim charm of this saint, with her plump, sallow cheeks and crinkled brown hair, I saw myself as I could have wished to be. I warmed to a loving sensitivity I had not hitherto suspected in him. Then he led me up a delicate spiral staircase to my bedroom; before she discreetly vanished, the housekeeper set him chuckling with some, I dare say, lewd blessing for newlyweds in her native Breton. That I did not understand. That he, smiling, refused to interpret.

And there lay the grand, hereditary matrimonial bed, itself the size, almost, of my little room at home, with the gargoyles carved on its surfaces of ebony, vermilion lacquer, gold leaf; and its white gauze curtains, billowing in the sea breeze. Our bed. And surrounded by so many mirrors! Mirrors on all the walls, in stately frames of contorted gold, that reflected more white lilies than I'd ever seen in my life before. He'd filled the room with them, to greet the bride, the young bride. The young bride, who had become that multitude of girls I saw in the mirrors, identical in their chic navy blue tailor-mades, for travelling, madame, or walking. A maid had dealt with the furs. Henceforth, a maid would deal with everything.

'See,' he said, gesturing towards those elegant girls. 'I have acquired a whole harem for myself!'

I found that I was trembling. My breath came thickly. I could not meet his eye and turned my head away, out of pride, out of shyness, and watched a dozen husbands approach me in a dozen mirrors and slowly, methodically, teasingly, unfasten the buttons of my jacket and slip it from my shoulders. Enough! No; more! Off comes the skirt; and, next, the blouse of apricot linen that cost more than the dress I had for first communion. The play of the waves outside in the cold sun glittered on his monocle; his movements seemed to me deliberately coarse, vulgar. The blood rushed to my face again, and stayed there.

And yet, you see, I guessed it might be so – that we should have a formal disrobing of the bride, a ritual from the brothel. Sheltered as my life had been, how could I have failed, even in the world of prim bohemia in which I lived, to have heard hints of *his* world?

He stripped me, gourmand that he was, as if he were stripping the leaves off an artichoke – but do not imagine much finesse about it; this artichoke was no particular treat for the diner nor was he yet in any greedy haste. He approached his familiar treat with a weary appetite. And when nothing but my scarlet, palpitating core remained, I saw, in the mirror, the living image of an etching by Rops from the collection he had shown me when our engagement permitted us to be alone together . . . the child with her sticklike limbs, naked but for her button boots, her gloves, shielding her face with her hand as though her face were the last repository of her modesty; and the old, monocled lecher who examined her, limb by limb. He in his London tailoring; she, bare as a lamb chop. Most pornographic of all confrontations. And so my purchaser unwrapped his bargain. And, as at the opera, when I had first seen my flesh in his eyes, I was aghast to feel myself stirring.

At once he closed my legs like a book and I saw again the rare movement of his lips that meant he smiled.

Not yet. Later. Anticipation is the greater part of pleasure, my little love.

And I began to shudder, like a racehorse before a race, yet also with a kind of fear, for I felt both a strange, impersonal arousal at the thought of love and at the same time a repugnance I could not stifle for his white, heavy flesh that had too much in common with the armfuls of arum lilies that filled my bedroom in great glass jars, those undertakers' lilies with the heavy pollen that powders your fingers as if you had dipped them in turmeric. The lilies I always associate with him; that are white. And stain you.

This scene from a voluptuary's life was now abruptly terminated. It turns out he has business to attend to; his estates, his companies – even on your honeymoon? Even then, said the red lips that kissed me before he left me alone with my bewildered senses – a wet, silken brush from his beard; a hint of the pointed tip of the tongue. Disgruntled, I wrapped a négligé of antique lace around me to sip the little breakfast of hot chocolate the maid brought me; after that, since it was second nature to me, there was nowhere to go but the music room and soon I settled down at my piano.

Yet only a series of subtle discords flowed from beneath my fingers: out of tune ... only a little out of tune; but I'd been blessed with perfect pitch and could not bear to play any more. Sea breezes are bad for pianos; we shall need a resident piano-tuner on the premises if I'm to continue with my studies! I flung down the lid in a little fury of disappointment; what should I do now, how shall I pass the long, sea-lit hours until my husband beds me?

I shivered to think of *that*.

His library seemed the source of his habitual odour of Russian leather. Row upon row of calf-bound volumes, brown and olive, with gilt lettering on their spines, the octavo in brilliant scarlet morocco. A deep-buttoned leather sofa to recline on. A lectern, carved like a spread eagle, that held open upon it an edition of Huysmans's *Là-bas*, from some over-exquisite private press; it had been bound like a missal, in brass, with gems of coloured glass. The rugs on the floor, deep, pulsing blues of heaven and red of the heart's dearest blood, came from Isfahan and Bokhara; the dark panelling gleamed; there was the lulling music of the sea and a fire of apple logs. The flames flickered along the spines inside a glass-fronted case that held books still crisp and new. Eliphas Levy; the name meant nothing to me. I squinted at a title or two: *The Initiation*, *The Key of Mysteries*, *The Secret of Pandora's Box*, and yawned. Nothing, here, to detain a seventeen-year-old girl waiting for her first embrace. I should have liked, best of all, a novel in yellow paper; I wanted to curl up on the rug before the blazing fire, lose myself in a cheap novel, munch sticky liqueur chocolates. If I rang for them, a maid would bring me chocolates.

Nevertheless, I opened the doors of that bookcase idly to browse. And I think I knew, I knew by some tingling of the fingertips, even before I opened that slim volume with no title at all on the spine, what I should find inside it. When he showed me the Rops, newly bought, dearly prized, had he not hinted that he was a connoisseur of such things? Yet I had not bargained for this, the girl with tears hanging on her cheeks like stuck pearls, her cunt a split fig below the great globes of her buttocks on which the knotted tails of the cat were about to descend, while a man in a black mask fingered with his free hand his prick, that curved upwards like the scimitar he held. The picture had a caption: 'Reproof of curiosity'. My mother, with all the precision of her eccentricity, had told me what it was that lovers did; I was innocent but not naïve. *The Adventures of Eulalie at the Harem of the Grand Turk* had been printed, according to the flyleaf, in Amsterdam in 1748, a rare collector's piece. Had some ancestor brought it back himself from that northern city? Or had my husband bought it for himself, from one of those dusty little bookshops on the Left Bank where an old man peers at you through spectacles an inch thick, daring you to inspect his wares ... I turned the pages in the anticipation of fear; the print was rusty. Here was another steel engraving: 'Immolation of the wives of the Sultan'. I knew enough for what I saw in that book to make me gasp.

There was a pungent intensification of the odour of leather that suffused his library; his shadow fell across the massacre.

'My little nun has found the prayerbooks, has she?' he demanded, with a curious mixture of mockery and relish; then, seeing my painful, furious bewilderment, he laughed at me aloud, snatched the book from my hands and put it down on the sofa.

'Have the nasty pictures scared Baby? Baby mustn't play with grownups' toys until she's learned how to handle them, must she?'

Then he kissed me. And with, this time, no reticence. He kissed me and laid his hand imperatively upon my breast, beneath the sheath of ancient lace. I stumbled on the winding stair that led to the bedroom, to the carved, gilded bed on which he had been conceived. I stammered foolishly: We've not taken luncheon yet; and, besides, it is broad daylight ...

All the better to see you.

He made me put on my choker, the family heirloom of one woman who had escaped the blade. With trembling fingers, I fastened the thing about my neck. It was cold as ice and chilled me. He twined my hair into a rope and lifted it off my shoulders so that he could the better kiss the downy furrows below my ears; that made me shudder. And he kissed those blazing rubies, too. He kissed them before he kissed my mouth. Rapt, he intoned: 'Of her apparel she retains/Only her sonorous jewellery.'

A dozen husbands impaled a dozen brides while the mewing gulls swung on invisible trapezes in the empty air outside.

I was brought to my senses by the insistent shrilling of the telephone. He lay beside me, felled like an oak, breathing stertorously, as if he had

17

been fighting with me. In the course of that one-sided struggle, I had seen his deathly composure shatter like a porcelain vase flung against a wall; I had heard him shriek and blaspheme at the orgasm; I had bled. And perhaps I had seen his face without its mask; and perhaps I had not. Yet I had been infinitely dishevelled by the loss of my virginity.

I gathered myself together, reached into the cloisonné cupboard beside the bed that concealed the telephone and addressed the mouthpiece. His agent in New York. Urgent.

I shook him awake and rolled over on my side, cradling my spent body in my arms. His voice buzzed like a hive of distant bees. My husband. My husband, who, with so much love, filled my bedroom with lilies until it looked like an embalming parlour. Those somnolent lilies, that wave their heavy heads, distributing their lush, insolent incense reminiscent of pampered flesh.

When he'd finished with the agent, he turned to me and stroked the ruby necklace that bit into my neck, but with such tenderness now, that I ceased flinching and he caressed my breasts. My dear one, my little love, my child, did it hurt her? He's so sorry for it, such impetuousness, he could not help himself; you see, he loves her so . . . and this lover's recitative of his brought my tears in a flood. I clung to him as though only the one who had inflicted the pain could comfort me for suffering it. For a while, he murmured to me in a voice I'd never heard before, a voice like the soft consolations of the sea. But then he unwound the tendrils of my hair from the buttons of his smoking jacket, kissed my cheek briskly and told me the agent from New York had called with such urgent business that he must leave as soon as the tide was low enough. Leave the castle? Leave France! And would be away for at least six weeks

'But it is our honeymoon!'

A deal, an enterprise of hazard and chance involving several millions, lay in the balance, he said. He drew away from me into that waxworks stillness of his; I was only a little girl, I did not understand. And, he said unspoken to my wounded vanity, I have had too many honeymoons to find them in the least pressing commitments. I know quite well that this child I've bought with a handful of coloured stones and the pelts of dead beasts won't run away. But, after he'd called his Paris agent to book a passage for the States next day – just one tiny call, my little one – we should have time for dinner together.

And I had to be content with that.

A Mexican dish of pheasant with hazelnuts and chocolate; salad;

white, voluptuous cheese; a sorbet of muscat grapes and Asti spumante. A celebration of Krug exploded festively. And then acrid black coffee in precious little cups so fine it shadowed the birds with which they were painted. I had cointreau, he had cognac in the library, with the purple velvet curtains drawn against the night, where he took me to perch on his knee in a leather armchair beside the flickering log fire. He had made me change into that chaste little Poiret shift of white muslin; he seemed especially fond of it, my breasts showed through the flimsy stuff, he said, like little soft white doves that sleep, each one, with a pink eye open. But he would not let me take off my ruby choker, although it was growing very uncomfortable, nor fasten up my descending hair, the sign of a virginity so recently ruptured that still remained a wounded presence between us. He twined his fingers in my hair until I winced; I said, I remember, very little.

'The maid will have changed our sheets already,' he said. 'We do not hang the bloody sheets out of the window to prove to the whole of Brittany you are a virgin, not in these civilized times. But I should tell you it would have been the first time in all my married lives I could have shown my interested tenants such a flag.'

Then I realized, with a shock of surprise, how it must have been my innocence that captivated him – the silent music, he said, of my unknowingness, like *La Terrasse des audiences au clair de lune* played upon a piano with keys of ether. You must remember how ill at ease I was in that luxurious place, how unease had been my constant companion during the whole length of my courtship by this grave satyr who now gently martyrized my hair. To know that my naïvety gave him some pleasure made me take heart. Courage! I shall act the fine lady to the manner born one day, if only by virtue of default.

Then, slowly yet teasingly, as if he were giving a child a great, mysterious treat, he took out a bunch of keys from some interior hidey-hole in his jacket – key after key, a key, he said, for every lock in the house. Keys of all kinds – huge, ancient things of black iron; others slender, delicate, almost baroque; wafer-thin Yale keys for safes and boxes. And, during his absence, it was I who must take care of them all.

I eyed the heavy bunch with circumspection. Until that moment, I had not given a single thought to the practical aspects of marriage with a great house, great wealth, a great man, whose key ring was as crowded as that of a prison warder. Here were the clumsy and archaic keys for the dungeons, for dungeons we had in plenty although they had been converted to cellars for his wines; the dusty bottles inhabited in racks all those deep holes of pain in the rock on which the castle was built. These are the keys to the kitchens, this is the key to the picture gallery, a treasure house filled by five centuries of avid collectors – ah! he foresaw I would spend hours there.

He had amply indulged his taste for the Symbolists, he told me with a glint of greed. There was Moreau's great portrait of his first wife, the famous *Sacrificial Victim* with the imprint of the lacelike chains on her pellucid skin. Did I know the story of the painting of that picture? How, when she took off her clothes for him for the first time, she fresh from her bar in Montmartre, she had robed herself involuntarily in a blush that reddened her breasts, her shoulders, her arms, her whole body? He had thought of that story, of that dear girl, when first he had undressed me ... Ensor, the great Ensor, his monolithic canvas: *The Foolish Virgins*. Two or three late Gauguins, his special favourite the one of the tranced brown girl in the deserted house which was called: *Out of the Night We Come, Into the Night We Go*. And, besides the additions he had made himself, his marvellous inheritance of Watteaus, Poussins and a pair of very special Fragonards, commissioned for a licentious ancestor who, it was said, had posed for the master's brush himself with his own two daughters ... He broke off his catalogue of treasures abruptly.

Your thin white face, chérie; he said, as if he saw it for the first time. Your thin white face, with its promise of debauchery only a connoisseur could detect.

A log fell in the fire, instigating a shower of sparks; the opal on my finger spurted green flame. I felt as giddy as if I were on the edge of a precipice; I was afraid, not so much of him, of his monstrous presence, heavy as if he had been gifted at birth with more specific *gravity* than the rest of us, the presence that, even when I thought myself most in love with him, always subtly oppressed me ... No. I was not afraid of him; but of myself. I seemed reborn in his unreflective eyes, reborn in unfamiliar shapes. I hardly recognized myself from his descriptions of me and yet, and yet – might there not be a grain of beastly truth in them? And, in the red firelight, I blushed again, unnoticed, to think he might have chosen me because, in my innocence, he sensed a rare talent for corruption.

Here is the key to the china cabinet – don't laugh, my darling; there's a king's ransom in Sèvres in that closet, and a queen's ransom in Limoges. And a key to the locked, barred room where five generations of plate were kept.

Keys, keys, keys. He would trust me with the keys to his office, although I was only a baby; and the keys to his safes, where he kept the jewels I should wear, he promised me, when we returned to Paris. Such jewels! Why, I would be able to change my earrings and necklaces three times a day, just as the Empress Josephine used to change her underwear. He doubted, he said, with that hollow, knocking sound that served him for a chuckle, I would be quite so interested in his share certificates although they, of course, were worth infinitely more.

Outside our firelit privacy, I could hear the sound of the tide drawing back from the pebbles of the foreshore; it was nearly time for him to leave me. One single key remained unaccounted for on the ring and he hesitated over it; for a moment, I thought he was going to unfasten it from its brothers, slip it back into his pocket and take it away with him.

'What is *that* key?' I demanded, for his chaffing had made me bold. 'The key to your heart? Give it me!'

He dangled the key tantalizingly above my head, out of reach of my straining fingers; those bare red lips of his cracked sidelong in a smile.

'Ah, no,' he said. 'Not the key to my heart. Rather, the key to my enfer.'

He left it on the ring, fastened the ring together, shook it musically, like a carillon. Then threw the keys in a jingling heap in my lap. I could feel the cold metal chilling my thighs through my thin muslin frock. He bent over me to drop a beard-masked kiss on my forehead.

'Every man must have one secret, even if only one, from his wife,' he said. 'Promise me this, my whey-faced piano-player; promise me you'll use all the keys on the ring except that last little one I showed you. Play with anything you find, jewels, silver plate; make toy boats of my share certificates, if it pleases you, and send them sailing off to America after me. All is yours, everywhere is open to you – except the lock that this single key fits. Yet all it is is the key to a little room at the foot of the west tower, behind the still-room, at the end of a dark little corridor full of horrid cobwebs that would get into your hair and frighten you if you ventured there. Oh, and you'd find it such a dull little room! But you must promise me, if you love me, to leave it well alone. It is only a private study, a hideaway, a "den", as the English say, where I can go, sometimes, on those infrequent yet inevitable occasions when the yoke of marriage seems to weigh too heavily on my shoulders. There I can go, you understand, to savour the rare pleasure of imagining myself wifeless.'

There was a little thin starlight in the courtyard as, wrapped in my furs, I saw him to his car. His last words were, that he had telephoned the mainland and taken a piano-tuner on to the staff; this man would arrive to take up his duties the next day. He pressed me to his vicuña breast, once, and then drove away.

I had drowsed away that afternoon and now I could not sleep. I lay tossing and turning in his ancestral bed until another daybreak discoloured the dozen mirrors that were iridescent with the reflections of the sea. The perfume of the lilies weighed on my senses; when I thought that, henceforth, I would always share these sheets with a man whose skin, as theirs did, contained that toad-like, clammy hint of moisture, I felt a vague desolation that within me, now my female wound had healed, there had awoken a certain queasy craving like the cravings of pregnant women for the taste of coal or chalk or tainted food, for the renewal of his caresses. Had he not hinted to me, in his flesh as in his speech and looks, of the thousand, thousand baroque intersections of flesh upon flesh? I lay in our wide bed accompanied by, a sleepless companion, my dark newborn curiosity.

I lay in bed alone. And I longed for him. And he disgusted me.

Were there jewels enough in all his safes to recompense me for this predicament? Did all that castle hold enough riches to recompense me for the company of the libertine with whom I must share it? And what, precisely, was the nature of my desirous dread for this mysterious being who, to show his mastery over me, had abandoned me on my wedding night?

Then I sat straight up in bed, under the sardonic masks of the gargoyles carved above me, riven by a wild surmise. Might he have left me, not for Wall Street but for an importunate mistress tucked away God knows where who knew how to pleasure him far better than a girl whose fingers had been exercised, hitherto, only by the practice of scales and arpeggios? And, slowly, soothed, I sank back on to the heaping pillows; I acknowledged that the jealous scare I'd just given myself was not unmixed with a little tincture of relief.

At last I drifted into slumber, as daylight filled the room and chased bad dreams away. But the last thing I remembered, before I slept, was the tall jar of lilies beside the bed, how the thick glass distorted their fat stems so they looked like arms, dismembered arms, drifting drowned in greenish water.

Coffee and croissants to console this bridal, solitary waking. Delicious. Honey, too, in a section of comb on a glass saucer. The maid squeezed the aromatic juice from an orange into a chilled goblet while I watched her as I lay in the lazy, midday bed of the rich. Yet nothing, this morning, gave me more than a fleeting pleasure except to hear that the piano-tuner had been at work already. When the maid told me that, I sprang out of bed and pulled on my old serge skirt and flannel blouse, costume of a student, in which I felt far more at ease with myself than in any of my fine new clothes.

After my three hours of practice, I called the piano-tuner in, to thank him. He was blind, of course; but young, with a gentle mouth and grey eyes that fixed upon me although they could not see me. He was a blacksmith's son from the village across the causeway; a chorister in the church whom the good priest had taught a trade so that he could make a living. All most satisfactory. Yes. He thought he would be happy here. And if, he added shyly, he might sometimes be allowed to hear me play . . . for, you see, he loved music. Yes. Of course, I said. Certainly. He seemed to know that I had smiled.

After I dismissed him, even though I'd woken so late, it was still barely time for my 'five o'clock'. The housekeeper, who, thoughtfully forewarned by my husband, had restrained herself from interrupting my music, now made me a solemn visitation with a lengthy menu for a late luncheon. When I told her I did not need it, she looked at me obliquely, along her nose. I understood at once that one of my principal functions as châtelaine was to provide work for the staff. But, all the same, I asserted myself and said I would wait until dinner-time, although I looked forward nervously to the solitary meal. Then I found I had to tell her what I would like to have prepared for me; my imagination, still that of a schoolgirl, ran riot. A fowl in cream – or should I anticipate Christmas with a varnished turkey? No; I have decided. Avocado and shrimp, lots of it, followed by no entrée at all. But surprise me for dessert with every ice-cream in the ice box. She noted all down but sniffed; I'd shocked her. Such tastes! Child that I was, I giggled when she left me.

But, now . . . what shall I do, now?

I could have spent a happy hour unpacking the trunks that contained my trousseau but the maid had done that already, the dresses, the tailor-mades hung in the wardrobe in my dressing room, the hats on wooden heads to keep their shape, the shoes on wooden feet as if all these inanimate objects were imitating the appearance of life, to mock me. I did not like to linger in my overcrowded dressing room, nor in my lugubriously lily-scented bedroom. How shall I pass the time?

I shall take a bath in my own bathroom! And found the taps were little dolphins made of gold, with chips of turquoise for eyes. And there was a tank of goldfish, who swam in and out of moving fronds of weeds, as bored, I thought, as I was. How I wished he had not left me. How I

wished it were possible to chat with, say, a maid; or, the piano-tuner
. . . but I knew already my new rank forbade overtures of friendship
to the staff.

I had been hoping to defer the call as long as I could, so that I
should have something to look forward to in the dead waste of time I
foresaw before me, after my dinner was done with, but, at a quarter
before seven, when darkness already surrounded the castle, I could
contain myself no longer. I telephoned my mother. And astonished
myself by bursting into tears when I heard her voice.

No, nothing was the matter. Mother, I have gold bath taps.

I said, gold bath taps!

No; I suppose that's nothing to cry about, Mother.

The line was bad, I could hardly make out her congratulations, her
questions, her concern, but I was a little comforted when I put the
receiver down.

Yet there still remained one whole hour to dinner and the whole,
unimaginable desert of the rest of the evening.

The bunch of keys lay, where he had left them, on the rug before
the library fire which had warmed their metal so that they no longer felt
cold to the touch but warm, almost, as my own skin. How careless I
was; a maid, tending the logs, eyed me reproachfully as if I'd set a trap
for her as I picked up the clinking bundle of keys, the keys to the
interior doors of this lovely prison of which I was both the inmate and
the mistress and had scarcely seen. When I remembered that, I felt the
exhilaration of the explorer.

Lights! More lights!

At the touch of a switch, the dreaming library was brilliantly
illuminated. I ran crazily about the castle, switching on every light I
could find – I ordered the servants to light up all their quarters, too, so
the castle would shine like a seaborne birthday cake lit with a thousand
candles, one for every year of its life, and everybody on shore would
wonder at it. When everything was lit as brightly as the café in the
Gare du Nord, the significance of the possessions implied by that
bunch of keys no longer intimidated me, for I was determined, now,
to search through them all for evidence of my husband's true nature.

His office first, evidently.

A mahogany desk half a mile wide, with an impeccable blotter and a
bank of telephones. I allowed myself the luxury of opening the safe
that contained the jewellery and delved sufficiently among the leather
boxes to find out how my marriage had given me access to a jinn's
treasury – parures, bracelets, rings . . . While I was thus surrounded by

diamonds, a maid knocked on the door and entered before I spoke; a subtle discourtesy. I would speak to my husband about it. She eyed my serge skirt superciliously; did madame plan to dress for dinner?

She made a moue of disdain when I laughed to hear that, she was far more the lady than I. But, imagine – to dress up in one of my Poiret extravaganzas, with the jewelled turban and aigrette on my head, roped with pearl to the navel, to sit down all alone in the baronial dining hall at the head of that massive board at which King Mark was reputed to have fed his knights . . . I grew calmer under the cold eye of her disapproval. I adopted the crisp inflections of an officer's daughter. No, I would not dress for dinner. Furthermore, I was not hungry enough for dinner itself. She must tell the housekeeper to cancel the dormitory feast I'd ordered. Could they leave me sandwiches and a flask of coffee in my music room? And would they all dismiss for the night?

Mais oui, madame.

I knew by her bereft intonation I had let them down again but I did not care; I was armed against them by the brilliance of his hoard. But I would not find his heart amongst the glittering stones; as soon as she had gone, I began a systematic search of the drawers of his desk.

All was in order, so I found nothing. Not a random doodle on an old envelope, nor the faded photograph of a woman. Only the files of business correspondence, the bills from the home farms, the invoices from tailors, the billets-doux from international financiers. Nothing. And this absence of the evidence of his real life began to impress me strangely; there must, I thought, be a great deal to conceal if he takes such pains to hide it.

His office was a singularly impersonal room, facing inwards, on to the courtyard, as though he wanted to turn his back on the siren sea in order to keep a clear head while he bankrupted a small businessman in Amsterdam or – I noticed with a thrill of distaste – engaged in some business in Laos that must, from certain cryptic references to his amateur botanist's enthusiasm for rare poppies, be to do with opium. Was he not rich enough to do without crime? Or was the crime itself his profit? And yet I saw enough to appreciate his zeal for secrecy.

Now I had ransacked his desk, I must spend a cool-headed quarter of an hour putting every last letter back where I had found it, and, as I covered the traces of my visit, by some chance, as I reached inside a little drawer that had stuck fast, I must have touched a hidden spring, for a secret drawer flew open within that drawer itself; and this secret drawer contained – at last! – a file marked: *Personal*.

I was alone, but for my reflection in the uncurtained window.

I had the brief notion that his heart, pressed flat as a flower, crimson and thin as tissue paper, lay in this file. It was a very thin one.

I could have wished, perhaps, I had not found that touching, ill-spelt note, on a paper napkin marked *La Coupole*, that began: 'My darling, I cannot wait for the moment when you may make me yours completely.' The diva had sent him a page of the score of *Tristan*, the Liebestod, with the single, cryptic word: 'Until . . .' scrawled across it. But the strangest of all these love letters was a postcard with a view of a village graveyard, among mountains, where some black-coated ghoul enthusiastically dug at a grave; this little scene, executed with the lurid exuberance of Grand Guignol, was captioned: 'Typical Transylvanian Scene – Midnight, All Hallows.' And, on the other side, the message: 'On the occasion of this marriage to the descendant of Dracula – always remember, "the supreme and unique pleasure of love is the certainty that one is doing evil". Toutes amitiés, C.'

A joke. A joke in the worst possible taste; for had he not been married to a Romanian countess? And then I remembered her pretty, witty face, and her name – Carmilla. My most recent predecessor in this castle had been, it would seem, the most sophisticated.

I put away the file, sobered. Nothing in my life of family love and music had prepared me for these grown-up games and yet these were clues to his self that showed me, at least, how much he had been loved, even if they did not reveal any good reason for it. But I wanted to know still more; and, as I closed the office door and locked it, the means to discover more fell in my way.

Fell, indeed; and with the clatter of a dropped canteen of cutlery, for, as I turned the slick Yale lock, I contrived, somehow, to open up the key ring itself, so that all the keys tumbled loose on the floor. And the very first key I picked out of that pile was, as luck or ill fortune had it, the key to the room he had forbidden me, the room he would keep for his own so that he could go there when he wished to feel himself once more a bachelor.

I made my decision to explore it before I felt a faint resurgence of my ill-defined fear of his waxen stillness. Perhaps I half-imagined, then, that I might find his real self in his den, waiting there to see if indeed I had obeyed him; that he had sent a moving figure of himself to New York, the enigmatic, self-sustaining carapace of his public person, while the real man, whose face I had glimpsed in the storm of orgasm, occupied himself with pressing private business in the study at the foot of the west tower, behind the still-room. Yet, if that were so, it was imperative that I should find him, should know him; and I was too deluded by his apparent taste for me to think my disobedience might truly offend him.

I took the forbidden key from the heap and left the others lying there.

It was now very late and the castle was adrift, as far as it could go from the land, in the middle of the silent ocean where, at my orders, it floated, like a garland of light. And all silent, all still, but for the murmuring of the waves.

I felt no fear, no intimation of dread. Now I walked as firmly as I had done in my mother's house.

Not a narrow, dusty little passage at all; why had he lied to me? But an ill-lit one, certainly; the electricity, for some reason, did not extend here, so I retreated to the still-room and found a bundle of waxed tapers in a cupboard, stored there with matches to light the oak board at grand dinners. I put a match to my little taper and advanced with it in my hand, like a penitent, along the corridor hung with heavy, I think Venetian, tapestries. The flame picked out, here, the head of a man, there, the rich breast of a woman spilling through a rent in her dress – the Rape of the Sabines, perhaps? The naked swords and immolated horses suggested some grisly mythological subject. The corridor wound downwards; there was an almost imperceptible ramp to the thickly carpeted floor. The heavy hangings on the wall muffled my footsteps, even my breathing. For some reason, it grew very warm; the sweat sprang out in beads on my brow. I could no longer hear the sound of the sea.

A long, a winding corridor, as if I were in the viscera of the castle; and this corridor led to a door of worm-eaten oak, low, round-topped, barred with black iron.

And still I felt no fear, no raising of the hairs on the back of the neck, no prickling of the thumbs.

The key slid into the new lock as easily as a hot knife into butter.

No fear; but a hesitation, a holding of the spiritual breath.

If I had found some traces of his heart in a file marked: *Personal*, perhaps, here, in his subterranean privacy, I might find a little of his soul. It was the consciousness of the possibility of such a discovery, of its possible strangeness, that kept me for a moment motionless, before, in the foolhardiness of my already subtly tainted innocence, I turned the key and the door creaked slowly back.

'There is a striking resemblance between the act of love and the ministrations of a torturer,' opined my husband's favourite poet; I had learned something of the nature of that similarity on my marriage bed. And now my taper showed me the outlines of a rack. There was also a great wheel, like the ones I had seen in woodcuts of the martyrdoms of the saints, in my old nurse's little store of holy books. And – just one glimpse of it before my little flame caved in and I was left in absolute darkness – a metal figure, hinged at the side, which I knew to be spiked on the inside and to have the name: the Iron Maiden. Absolute darkness. And, about me, the instruments of mutilation.

Until that moment, this spoiled child did not know she had inherited nerves and a will from the mother who had defied the yellow outlaws of Indo-China. My mother's spirit drove me on, into that dreadful place, in a cold ecstasy to know the very worst. I fumbled for the matches in my pocket; what a dim, lugubrious light they gave! And yet, enough, oh, more than enough, to see a room designed for desecration and some dark night of unimaginable lovers whose embraces were annihilation.

The walls of this stark torture chamber were the naked rock; they gleamed as if they were sweating with fright. At the four corners of the room were funerary urns, of great antiquity, Etruscan, perhaps, and, on three-legged ebony stands, the bowls of incense he had left burning which filled the room with a sacerdotal reek. Wheel, rack and Iron Maiden were, I saw, displayed as grandly as if they were items of statuary and I was almost consoled, then, and almost persuaded myself that I might have stumbled only upon a little museum of his perversity, that he had installed these monstrous items here only for contemplation.

Yet at the centre of the room lay a catafalque, a doomed, ominous bier of Renaissance workmanship, surrounded by long white candles and, at its foot, an armful of the same lilies with which he had filled my bedroom, stowed in a four-foot-high jar glazed with a sombre Chinese red. I scarcely dared examine this catafalque and its occupant more closely; yet I knew I must.

Each time I struck a match to light those candles round her bed, it seemed a garment of that innocence of mine for which he had lusted fell away from me.

The opera singer lay, quite naked, under a thin sheet of very rare and precious linen, such as the princes of Italy used to shroud those whom they had poisoned. I touched her, very gently, on the white breast; she was cool, he had embalmed her. On her throat I could see the blue imprint of his strangler's fingers. The cool, sad flame of the candles flickered on her white, closed eyelids. The worst thing was, the dead lips smiled.

Beyond the catafalque, in the middle of the shadows, a white, nacreous glimmer; as my eyes accustomed themselves to the gathering darkness, I at last – oh, horrors! – made out a skull; yes, a skull, so utterly denuded, now, of flesh, that it scarcely seemed possible the stark bone had once been richly upholstered with life. And this skull was strung up by a system of unseen cords, so that it appeared to hang, disembodied, in the still, heavy air, and it had been crowned with a wreath of white roses, and a veil of lace, the final image of his bride.

Yet the skull was still so beautiful, had shaped with its sheer planes so imperiously the face that had once existed above it, that I recognized her the moment I saw her; face of the evening star walking on the rim of night. One false step, oh, my poor, dear girl, next in the fated sister-hood of his wives; one false step and into the abyss of the dark you stumbled.

And where was she, the latest dead, the Romanian countess who might have thought her blood would survive his depredations? I knew she must be here, in the place that had wound me through the castle towards it on a spool of inexorability. But, at first, I could see no sign of her. Then, for some reason – perhaps some change of atmosphere wrought by my presence – the metal shell of the Iron Maiden emitted a ghostly twang; my feverish imagination might have guessed its occu-pant was trying to clamber out, though, even in the midst of my rising hysteria, I knew she must be dead to find a home there.

With trembling fingers, I prised open the front of the upright coffin, with its sculpted face caught in a rictus of pain. Then, overcome, I dropped the key I still held in my other hand. It dropped into the forming pool of her blood.

She was pierced, not by one but by a hundred spikes, this child of the land of the vampires who seemed so newly dead, so full of blood ... oh God! how recently had he become a widower? How long had he kept her in this obscene cell? Had it been all the time he had courted me, in the clear light of Paris?

I closed the lid of her coffin very gently and burst into a tumult of sobbing that contained both pity for his other victims and also a dread-ful anguish to know I, too, was one of them.

The candles flared, as if in a draught from a door to elsewhere. The light caught the fire opal on my hand so that it flashed, once, with a baleful light, as if to tell me the eye of God – his eye – was upon me. My first thought, when I saw the ring for which I had sold myself to this fate, was, how to escape it.

I retained sufficient presence of mind to snuff out the candles round the bier with my fingers, to gather up my taper, to look around, al-though shuddering, to ensure I had left behind me no traces of my visit.

I retrieved the key from the pool of blood, wrapped it in my handkerchief to keep my hands clean, and fled the room, slamming the door behind me.

It crashed to with a juddering reverberation, like the door of hell.

I could not take refuge in my bedroom, for that retained the memory of his presence trapped in the fathomless silvering of his mirrors. My music room seemed the safest place, although I looked at the picture of Saint Cecilia with a faint dread; what had been the nature of her martyrdom? My mind was in a tumult; schemes for flight jostled with one another . . . as soon as the tide receded from the causeway, I would make for the mainland – on foot, running, stumbling; I did not trust that leather-clad chauffeur, nor the well-behaved housekeeper, and I dared not take any of the pale, ghostly maids into my confidence, either, since they were his creatures, all. Once at the village, I would fling myself directly on the mercy of the gendarmerie.

But – could I trust them, either? His forefathers had ruled this coast for eight centuries, from this castle whose moat was the Atlantic. Might not the police, the advocates, even the judge, all be in his service, turning a common blind eye to his vices since he was milord whose word must be obeyed? Who, on this distant coast, would believe the white-faced girl from Paris who came running to them with a shuddering tale of blood, of fear, of the ogre murmuring in the shadows? Or, rather, they would immediately know it to be true. But were all honour-bound to let me carry it no further.

Assistance. My mother. I ran to the telephone; and the line, of course, was dead.

Dead as his wives.

A thick darkness, unlit by any star, still glazed the windows. Every lamp in my room burned, to keep the dark outside, yet it seemed still to encroach on me, to be present beside me but as if masked by my lights, the night like a permeable substance that could seep into my skin. I looked at the precious little clock made from hypocritically innocent flowers long ago, in Dresden; the hands had scarcely moved one single hour forward from when I first descended to that private slaughterhouse of his. Time was his servant, too; it would trap me, here, in a night that would last until he came back to me, like a black sun on a hopeless morning.

And yet the time might still be my friend; at that hour, that very hour, he set sail for New York.

To know that, in a few moments, my husband would have left France calmed my agitation a little. My reason told me I had nothing to fear; the tide that would take him away to the New World would let me out of the imprisonment of the castle. Surely I could easily evade the servants. Anybody can buy a ticket at a railway station. Yet I was still filled with unease. I opened the lid of the piano; perhaps I thought my own particular magic might help me, now, that I could create a pentacle out of music that would keep me from harm for, if my music had first ensnared him, then might it not also give me the power to free myself from him?

Mechanically, I began to play but my fingers were stiff and shaking. At first, I could manage nothing better than the exercises of Czerny but simply the act of playing soothed me and, for solace, for the sake of the harmonious rationality of its sublime mathematics, I searched among his scores until I found *The Well-Tempered Clavier*. I set myself the therapeutic task of playing all Bach's equations, every one, and, I told myself, if I played them all through without a single mistake – then the morning would find me once more a virgin.

Crash of a dropped stick.

His silver-headed cane! What else? Sly, cunning, he had returned; he was waiting for me outside the door!

I rose to my feet; fear gave me strength. I flung back my head defiantly.

'Come in!' My voice astonished me by its firmness, its clarity.

The door slowly, nervously opened and I saw, not the massive, irredeemable bulk of my husband but the slight, stooping figure of the piano-tuner, and he looked far more terrified of me than my mother's daughter would have been of the Devil himself. In the torture chamber, it seemed to me that I would never laugh again; now, helplessly, laugh I did, with relief, and, after a moment's hesitation, the boy's face softened and he smiled a little, almost in shame. Though they were blind, his eyes were singularly sweet.

'Forgive me,' said Jean-Yves. 'I know I've given you grounds for dismissing me, that I should be crouching outside your door at midnight ... but I heard you walking about, up and down – I sleep in a room at the foot of the west tower – and some intuition told me you could not sleep and might, perhaps, pass the insomniac hours at your piano. And I could not resist that. Besides, I stumbled over these –'

And he displayed the ring of keys I'd dropped outside my husband's office door, the ring from which one key was missing. I took them from him, looked round for a place to stow them, fixed on the piano stool as if to hide them would protect me. Still he stood smiling at me. How hard it was to make everyday conversation.

'It's perfect,' I said. 'The piano. Perfectly in tune.'

But he was full of the loquacity of embarrassment, as though I would only forgive him for his impudence if he explained the cause of it thoroughly.

'When I heard you play this afternoon, I thought I'd never heard such a touch. Such technique. A treat for me, to hear a virtuoso! So I crept up to your door now, humbly as a little dog might, madame, and put my ear to the keyhole and listened, and listened – until my stick fell to the floor through a momentary clumsiness of mine, and I was discovered.'

He had the most touchingly ingenuous smile.

'Perfectly in tune,' I repeated. To my surprise, now I had said it, I found I could not say anything else. I could only repeat: 'In tune . . . perfect . . . in tune,' over and over again. I saw a dawning surprise in his face. My head throbbed. To see him, in his lovely, blind humanity, seemed to hurt me very piercingly, somewhere inside my breast; his figure blurred, the room swayed about me. After the dreadful revelation of that bloody chamber, it was his tender look that made me faint.

When I recovered consciousness, I found I was lying in the piano-tuner's arms and he was tucking the satin cushion from the piano-stool under my head.

'You are in some great distress,' he said. 'No bride should suffer so much, so early in her marriage.'

His speech had the rhythms of the countryside, the rhythms of the tides.

'Any bride brought to this castle should come ready dressed in mourning, should bring a priest and a coffin with her,' I said.

'What's this?'

It was too late to keep silent; and if he, too, were one of my husband's creatures, then at least he had been kind to me. So I told him everything, the keys, the interdiction, my disobedience, the room, the rack, the skull, the corpses, the blood.

'I can scarcely believe it,' he said, wondering. 'That man . . . so rich; so well-born.'

'Here's proof,' I said and tumbled the fatal key out of my handkerchief on to the silken rug.

'Oh God,' he said. 'I can smell the blood.'

He took my hand; he pressed his arms about me. Although he was scarcely more than a boy, I felt a great strength flow into me from his touch.

'We whisper all manner of strange tales up and down the coast,' he said. 'There was a Marquis, once, who used to hunt young girls on the mainland; he hunted them with dogs, as though they were foxes. My grandfather had it from his grandfather, how the Marquis pulled a head out of his saddle bag and showed it to the blacksmith while the man was shoeing his horse. "A fine specimen of the genus, brunette, eh, Guillaume?" And it was the head of the blacksmith's wife.'

But, in these more democratic times, my husband must travel as far as Paris to do his hunting in the salons. Jean-Yves knew the moment I shuddered.

'Oh, madame! I thought all these were old wives' tales, chattering of fools, spooks to scare bad children into good behaviour! Yet how could you know, a stranger, that the old name for this place is the Castle of Murder?'

How could I know, indeed? Except that, in my heart, I'd always known its lord would be the death of me.

'Hark!' said my friend suddenly. 'The sea has changed key; it must be near morning, the tide is going down.'

He helped me up. I looked from the window, towards the mainland, along the causeway where the stones gleamed wetly in the thin light of the end of the night and, with an almost unimaginable horror, a horror the intensity of which I cannot transmit to you, I saw, in the distance, still far away yet drawing moment by moment inexorably nearer, the twin headlamps of his great black car, gouging tunnels through the shifting mist.

My husband had indeed returned; this time, it was no fancy.

'The key!' said Jean-Yves. 'It must go back on the ring, with the others. As though nothing had happened.'

But the key was still caked with wet blood and I ran to my bathroom and held it under the hot tap. Crimson water swirled down the basin but, as if the key itself were hurt, the bloody token stuck. The turquoise eyes of the dolphin taps winked at me derisively; they knew my husband had been too clever for me! I scrubbed the stain with my nail brush but still it would not budge. I thought how the car would be rolling silently towards the closed courtyard gate; the more I scrubbed the key, the more vivid grew the stain.

The bell in the gatehouse would jangle. The porter's drowsy son would push back the patchwork quilt, yawning, pull the shirt over his head, thrust his feet into his sabots ... slowly, slowly; open the door for your master as slowly as you can ...

And still the bloodstain mocked the fresh water that spilled from the mouth of the leering dolphin.

'You have no more time,' said Jean-Yves. 'He is here. I know it. I must stay with you.'

'You shall not!' I said. 'Go back to your room, now. Please.'

He hesitated. I put an edge of steel in my voice, for I knew I must meet my lord alone.

'Leave me!'

As soon as he had gone, I dealt with the keys and went to my bedroom. The causeway was empty; Jean-Yves was correct, my husband had already entered the castle. I pulled the curtains close, stripped off my clothes and pulled the bedcurtains round me as a pungent aroma of Russian leather assured me my husband was once again beside me.

'Dearest!'

With the most treacherous, lascivious tenderness, he kissed my eyes, and, mimicking the new bride newly wakened, I flung my arms around him, for on my seeming acquiescence depended my salvation.

'Da Silva of Rio outwitted me,' he said wryly. 'My New York agent telegraphed Le Havre and saved me a wasted journey. So we may resume our interrupted pleasures, my love.'

I did not believe one word of it. I knew I had behaved exactly according to his desires; had he not bought me so that I should do so? I had been tricked into my own betrayal to that illimitable darkness whose source I had been compelled to seek in his absence and, now that I had met that shadowed reality of his that came to life only in the presence of its own atrocities, I must pay the price of my new knowledge. The secret of Pandora's box; but he had given me the box, himself, knowing I must learn the secret. I had played a game in which every move was governed by a destiny as oppressive and omnipotent as himself, since that destiny was himself; and I had lost. Lost at that charade of innocence and vice in which he had engaged me. Lost, as the victim loses to the executioner.

His hand brushed my breast, beneath the sheet. I strained my nerves yet could not help but flinch from the intimate touch, for it made me think of the piercing embrace of the Iron Maiden and of his lost lovers in the vault. When he saw my reluctance, his eyes veiled over and yet his appetite did not diminish. His tongue ran over red lips already wet. Silent, mysterious, he moved away from me to draw off his jacket. He took the gold watch from his waistcoat and laid it on the dressing table, like a good bourgeois; scooped out his rattling loose change and now – oh God! – makes a great play of patting his pockets officiously, puzzled lips pursed, searching for something that has been mislaid. Then turns to me with a ghastly, a triumphant smile.

'But of course! I gave the keys to you!'

'Your keys? Why, of course. Here, they're under the pillow; wait a moment – what – Ah! No . . . now, where can I have left them? I was whiling away the evening without you at the piano, I remember. Of course! The music room!'

Brusquely he flung my négligé of antique lace on the bed.

'Go and get them.'

'Now? This moment? Can't it wait until morning, my darling?'

I forced myself to be seductive. I saw myself, pale, pliant as a plant that begs to be trampled underfoot, a dozen vulnerable, appealing girls reflected in as many mirrors, and I saw how he almost failed to resist me. If he had come to me in bed, I would have strangled him, then.

But he half-snarled: 'No. It won't wait. Now.'

The unearthly light of dawn filled the room; had only one previous dawn broken upon me in that vile place? And there was nothing for it but to go and fetch the keys from the music stool and pray he would not examine them too closely, pray to God his eyes would fail him, that he might be struck blind.

When I came back into the bedroom carrying the bunch of keys that jangled at every step like a curious musical instrument, he was sitting on the bed in his immaculate shirtsleeves, his head sunk in his hands.

And it seemed to me he was in despair.

Strange. In spite of my fear of him, that made me whiter than my wrap, I felt there emanate from him, at that moment, a stench of absolute despair, rank and ghastly, as if the lilies that surrounded him had all at once begun to fester, or the Russian leather of his scent were reverting to the elements of flayed hide and excrement of which it was composed. The chthonic gravity of his presence exerted a tremendous pressure on the room, so that the blood pounded in my ears as if we had been precipitated to the bottom of the sea, beneath the waves that pounded against the shore.

I held my life in my hands amongst those keys and, in a moment, would place it between his well-manicured fingers. The evidence of that bloody chamber had showed me I could expect no mercy. Yet, when he raised his head and stared at me with his blind, shuttered eyes as though he did not recognize me, I felt a terrified pity for him, for this man who lived in such strange, secret places that, if I loved him enough to follow him, I should have to die.

The atrocious loneliness of that monster!

The monocle had fallen from his face. His curling mane was disordered, as if he had run his hands through it in his distraction. I saw how he had lost his impassivity and was now filled with suppressed excitement. The hand he stretched out for those counters in his game of love and death shook a little; the face that turned towards me contained a sombre delirium that seemed to me compounded of a ghastly, yes, shame but also of a terrible, guilty joy as he slowly ascertained how I had sinned.

That tell-tale stain had resolved itself into a mark the shape and brilliance of the heart on a playing card. He disengaged the key from the ring and looked at it for a while, solitary, brooding.

'It is the key that leads to the kingdom of the unimaginable,' he said. His voice was low and had in it the timbre of certain great cathedral organs that seem, when they are played, to be conversing with God.

I could not restrain a sob.

'Oh, my love, my little love who brought me a white gift of music,' he said, almost as if grieving. 'My little love, you'll never know how much I hate daylight!'

Then he sharply ordered: 'Kneel!'

I knelt before him and he pressed the key lightly to my forehead, held it there for a moment. I felt a faint tingling of the skin and, when I involuntarily glanced at myself in the mirror, I saw the heart-shaped stain had transferred itself to my forehead, to the space between the eyebrows, like the caste mark of a brahmin woman. Or the mark of Cain. And now the key gleamed as freshly as if it had just been cut. He clipped it back on the ring, emitting that same, heavy sigh as he had done when I said that I would marry him.

'My virgin of the arpeggios, prepare yourself for martyrdom.'

'What form shall it take?' I said.

'Decapitation,' he whispered, almost voluptuously. 'Go and bathe yourself; put on that white dress you wore to hear *Tristan* and the necklace that prefigures your end. And I shall take myself off to the armoury, my dear, to sharpen my great-grandfather's ceremonial sword.'

'The servants?'

'We shall have absolute privacy for our last rites; I have already dismissed them. If you look out of the window you can see them going to the mainland.'

It was now the full, pale light of morning; the weather was grey, indeterminate, the sea had an oily, sinister look, a gloomy day on which to die. Along the causeway I could see trouping every maid and scullion, every pot-boy and pan-scourer, valet, laundress and vassal who worked in that great house, most on foot, a few on bicycles. The faceless housekeeper trudged along with a great basket in which, I guessed, she'd stowed as much as she could ransack from the larder. The Marquis must have given the chauffeur leave to borrow the motor for the day, for it went last of all, at a stately pace, as though the procession were a cortège and the car already bore my coffin to the mainland for burial.

But I knew no good Breton earth would cover me, like a last, faithful lover; I had another fate.

'I have given them all a day's holiday, to celebrate our wedding,' he said. And smiled.

However hard I stared at the receding company, I could see no sign of Jean-Yves, our latest servant, hired but the preceding morning.

'Go, now. Bathe yourself; dress yourself. The lustratory ritual and the ceremonial robing; after that, the sacrifice. Wait in the music room until I telephone for you. No, my dear!' And he smiled, as I started, recalling the line was dead. 'One may call inside the castle just as much as one pleases; but, outside – never.'

I scrubbed my forehead with the nail brush as I had scrubbed the key but this red mark would not go away, either, no matter what I did, and I knew I should wear it until I died, though that would not be long. Then I went to my dressing room and put on that white muslin shift, costume of a victim of an auto-da-fé, he had bought me to listen to the Liebestod in. Twelve young women combed out twelve listless sheaves of brown hair in the mirrors; soon, there would be none. The mass of lilies that surrounded me exhaled, now, the odour of their withering. They looked like the trumpets of the angels of death.

On the dressing table, coiled like a snake about to strike, lay the ruby choker.

Already almost lifeless, cold at heart, I descended the spiral staircase to the music room but there I found I had not been abandoned.

'I can be of some comfort to you,' the boy said. 'Though not much use.'

We pushed the piano stool in front of the open window so that, for as long as I could, I would be able to smell the ancient, reconciling smell of the sea that, in time, will cleanse everything, scour the old bones white, wash away all the stains. The last little chambermaid had trotted along the causeway long ago and now the tide, fated as I, came tumbling in, the crisp wavelets splashing on the old stones.

'You do not deserve this,' he said.

'Who can say what I deserve or no?' I said. 'I've done nothing; but that may be sufficient reason for condemning me.'

'You disobeyed him,' he said. 'That is sufficient reason for him to punish you.'

'I only did what he knew I would.'

'Like Eve,' he said.

The telephone rang a shrill imperative. Let it ring. But my lover lifted me up and set me on my feet; I knew I must answer it. The receiver felt heavy as earth.

'The courtyard. Immediately.'

My lover kissed me, he took my hand. He would come with me if I would lead him. Courage. When I thought of courage, I thought of my mother. Then I saw a muscle in my lover's face quiver.

'Hoofbeats!' he said.

I cast one last, desperate glance from the window and, like a miracle, I saw a horse and rider galloping at a vertiginous speed along the causeway, though the waves crashed, now, high as the horse's fetlocks. A rider, her black skirts tucked up around her waist so she could ride hard and fast, a crazy, magnificent horsewoman in widow's weeds.

As the telephone rang again.

'Am I to wait all morning?'

Every moment, my mother drew nearer.

'She will be too late,' Jean-Yves said and yet he could not restrain a note of hope that, though it must be so, yet it might not be so.

The third, intransigent call.

'Shall I come up to heaven to fetch you down, Saint Cecilia? You wicked woman, do you wish me to compound my crimes by desecrating the marriage bed?'

So I must go to the courtyard where my husband waited in his London-tailored trousers and the shirt from Turnbull and Asser, beside the mounting block, with, in his hand, the sword which his great-grandfather had presented to the little corporal, in token of surrender to the Republic, before he shot himself. The heavy sword, unsheathed, grey as that November morning, sharp as childbirth, mortal.

When my husband saw my companion, he observed: 'Let the blind lead the blind, eh? But does even a youth as besotted as you are think she was truly blind to her own desires when she took my ring? Give it me back, whore.'

The fires in the opal had all died down. I gladly slipped it from my finger and, even in that dolorous place, my heart was lighter for the lack of it. My husband took it lovingly and lodged it on the tip of his little finger; it would go no further.

'It will serve me for a dozen more fiancées,' he said. 'To the block, woman. No – leave the boy; I shall deal with him later, utilizing a less exalted instrument than the one with which I do my wife the honour of her immolation, for do not fear that in death you will be divided.'

Slowly, slowly, one foot before the other, I crossed the cobbles. The longer I dawdled over my execution, the more time it gave the avenging angel to descend . . .

'Don't loiter, girl! Do you think I shall lose appetite for the meal if you are so long about serving it? No; I shall grow hungrier, more ravenous with each moment, more cruel . . . Run to me, run! I have a place prepared for your exquisite corpse in my display of flesh!'

He raised the sword and cut bright segments from the air with it, but still I lingered although my hopes, so recently raised, now began to flag. If she is not here by now, her horse must have stumbled on the causeway, have plunged into the sea . . . One thing only made me glad; that my lover would not see me die.

My husband laid my branded forehead on the stone and, as he had done once before, twisted my hair into a rope and drew it away from my neck.

'Such a pretty neck,' he said with what seemed to be a genuine, retrospective tenderness. 'A neck like the stem of a young plant.'

I felt the silken bristle of his beard and the wet touch of his lips as he kissed my nape. And, once again, of my apparel I must retain only my gems; the sharp blade ripped my dress in two and it fell from me. A little green moss, growing in the crevices of the mounting block, would be the last thing I should see in all the world.

The whizz of that heavy sword.

And – a great battering and pounding at the gate, the jangling of the bell, the frenzied neighing of a horse! The unholy silence of the place shattered in an instant. The blade did *not* descend, the necklace did *not* sever, my head did *not* roll. For, for an instant, the beast wavered in his stroke, a sufficient split second of astonished indecision to let me spring upright and dart to the assistance of my lover as he struggled sightlessly with the great bolts that kept her out.

The Marquis stood transfixed, utterly dazed, at a loss. It must have been as if he had been watching his beloved *Tristan* for the twelfth, the thirteenth time and Tristan stirred, then leapt from his bier in the last act, announced in a jaunty aria interposed from Verdi that bygones were bygones, crying over spilt milk did nobody any good and, as for himself, he proposed to live happily ever after. The puppet master, open-mouthed, wide-eyed, impotent at the last, saw his dolls break free of their strings, abandon the rituals he had ordained for them since time began and start to live for themselves; the king, aghast, witnesses the revolt of his pawns.

You never saw such a wild thing as my mother, her hat seized by the winds and blown out to sea so that her hair was her white mane, her

39

black lisle legs exposed to the thigh, her skirts tucked round her waist, one hand on the reins of the rearing horse while the other clasped my father's service revolver and, behind her, the breakers of the savage, indifferent sea, like the witnesses of a furious justice. And my husband stood stock-still, as if she had been Medusa, the sword still raised over his head as in those clockwork tableaux of Bluebeard that you see in glass cases at fairs.

And then it was as though a curious child pushed his centime into the slot and set all in motion. The heavy, bearded figure roared out aloud, braying with fury, and, wielding the honourable sword as if it were a matter of death or glory, charged us, all three.

On her eighteenth birthday, my mother had disposed of a man-eating tiger that had ravaged the villages in the hills north of Hanoi. Now, without a moment's hesitation, she raised my father's gun, took aim and put a single, irreproachable bullet through my husband's head.

We lead a quiet life, the three of us. I inherited, of course, enormous wealth but we have given most of it away to various charities. The castle is now a school for the blind, though I pray that the children who live there are not haunted by any sad ghosts looking for, crying for, the husband who will never return to the bloody chamber, the contents of which are buried or burned, the door sealed.

I felt I had a right to retain sufficient funds to start a little music school here, on the outskirts of Paris, and we do well enough. Sometimes we can even afford to go to the Opéra, though never to sit in a box, of course. We know we are the source of many whisperings and much gossip but the three of us know the truth of it and mere chatter can never harm us. I can only bless the – what shall I call it? – the *maternal telepathy* that sent my mother running headlong from the telephone to the station after I had called her, that night. I never heard you cry before, she said, by way of explanation. Not when you were happy. And who ever cried because of gold bath taps?

The night train, the one I had taken; she lay in her berth, sleepless as I had been. When she could not find a taxi at that lonely halt, she borrowed old Dobbin from a bemused farmer, for some internal urgency told her that she must reach me before the incoming tide sealed me away from her for ever. My poor old nurse, left scandalized at home – what? interrupt milord on his honeymoon? – she died soon after. She had taken so much secret pleasure in the fact that her little girl had become a marquise; and now here I was, scarcely a penny the richer, widowed at seventeen in the most dubious circumstances and busily engaged in setting up house with a piano-tuner. Poor thing, she passed away in a sorry state of disillusion! But I do believe my mother loves him as much as I do.

No paint nor powder, no matter how thick or white, can mask that red mark on my forehead; I am glad he cannot see it – not for fear of his revulsion, since I know he sees me clearly with his heart – but, because it spares my shame.

The Courtship of Mr Lyon

Outside her kitchen window, the hedgerow glistened as if the snow possessed a light of its own; when the sky darkened towards evening, an unearthly, reflected pallor remained behind upon the winter's landscape, while still the soft flakes floated down. This lovely girl, whose skin possesses that same, inner light so you would have thought she, too, was made all of snow, pauses in her chores in the mean kitchen to look out at the country road. Nothing has passed that way all day; the road is white and unmarked as a spilled bolt of bridal satin.

Father said he would be home before nightfall.

The snow brought down all the telephone wires; he couldn't have called, even with the best of news.

The roads are bad. I hope he'll be safe.

But the old car stuck fast in a rut, wouldn't budge an inch; the engine whirred, coughed and died and he was far from home. Ruined, once; then ruined again, as he had learnt from his lawyers that very morning; at the conclusion of the lengthy, slow attempt to restore his fortunes, he had turned out his pockets to find the cash for petrol to take him home. And not even enough money left over to buy his Beauty, his girl-child, his pet, the one white rose she said she wanted; the only gift she wanted, no matter how the case went, how rich he might once again be. She had asked for so little and he had not been able to give it to her. He cursed the useless car, the last straw that broke his spirit; then, nothing for it but to fasten his old sheepskin coat around him, abandon the heap of metal and set off down the snow-filled lane to look for help.

Behind wrought iron gates, a short, snowy drive performed a reticent flourish before a miniature, perfect, Palladian house that seemed to hide itself shyly behind snow-laden skirts of an antique cypress. It was almost night; that house, with its sweet, retiring melancholy grace, would have seemed deserted but for a light that flickered in an upstairs window, so vague it might have been the reflection of a star, if any stars could have penetrated the snow that whirled yet more thickly. Chilled through, he pressed the latch of the gate and saw, with a pang, how, on the withered ghost of a tangle of thorns, there clung, still, the faded rag of a white rose.

The gate clanged loudly shut behind him; too loudly. For an instant, that reverberating clang seemed final, emphatic, ominous as if the gate, now closed, barred all within it from the world outside the walled, wintry garden. And, from a distance, though from what distance he could not tell, he heard the most singular sound in the world: a great roaring, as of a beast of prey.

In too much need to allow himself to be intimidated, he squared up to the mahogany door. This door was equipped with a knocker in the shape of a lion's head, with a ring through the nose; as he raised his hand towards it, it came to him this lion's head was not, as he had thought at first, made of brass, but, instead, of solid gold. Before, however, he could announce his presence, the door swung silently inward on well-oiled hinges and he saw a white hall where the candles of a great chandelier cast their benign light upon so many, many flowers in great, free-standing jars of crystal that it seemed the whole of spring drew him into its warmth with a profound intake of perfumed breath. Yet there was no living person in the hall.

The door behind him closed as silently as it had opened, yet, this time, he felt no fear although he knew by the pervasive atmosphere of a suspension of reality that he had entered a place of privilege where all the laws of the world he knew need not necessarily apply, for the very rich are often very eccentric and the house was plainly that of an exceedingly wealthy man. As it was, when nobody came to help him with his coat, he took it off himself. At that, the crystals of the chandelier tinkled a little, as if emitting a pleased chuckle, and the door of a cloakroom opened of its own accord. There were, however, no clothes at all in this cloakroom, not even the statutory country-house garden mackintosh to greet his own squirearchal sheepskin, but, when he emerged again into the hall, he found a greeting waiting for him at last – there was, of all things, a liver and white King Charles spaniel crouched, with head intelligently cocked, on the Kelim runner. It gave him further, comforting proof of his unseen host's wealth and eccentricity to see the dog wore, in place of a collar, a diamond necklace.

The dog sprang to its feet in welcome and busily shepherded him (how amusing!) to a snug little leather-panelled study on the first floor, where a low table was drawn up to a roaring log fire. On the table, a silver tray; round the neck of the whisky decanter, a silver tag with the legend: *Drink me*, while the cover of the silver dish was engraved with the exhortation: *Eat me*, in a flowing hand. This dish contained sandwiches of thick-cut roast beef, still bloody. He drank the one with soda and ate the other with some excellent mustard thoughtfully provided in a stoneware pot, and, when the spaniel saw to it he had served himself, she trotted off about her own business.

All that remained to make Beauty's father entirely comfortable was to find, in a curtained recess, not only a telephone but the card of a garage that advertised a twenty-four-hour rescue service; a couple of calls later and he had confirmed, thank God, there was no serious trouble, only the car's age and the cold weather . . . could he pick it up from the village in an hour? And directions to the village, but half a mile away, were supplied, in a new tone of deference, as soon as he described the house from where he was calling.

And he was disconcerted but, in his impecunious circumstances, relieved to hear the bill would go on his hospitable if absent host's account; no question, assured the mechanic. It was the master's custom.

Time for another whisky as he tried, unsuccessfully, to call Beauty and tell her he would be late; but the lines were still down, although, miraculously, the storm had cleared as the moon rose and now a glance between the velvet curtains revealed a landscape as of ivory with an inlay of silver. Then the spaniel appeared again, with his hat in her careful mouth, prettily wagging her tail, as if to tell him it was time to be gone, that this magical hospitality was over.

As the door swung to behind him, he saw the lion's eyes were made of agate.

Great wreaths of snow now precariously curded the rose trees and, when he brushed against a stem on his way to the gate, a chill armful softly thudded to the ground to reveal, as if miraculously preserved

43

beneath it, one last, single, perfect rose that might have been the last rose left living in all the white winter, and of so intense and yet delicate a fragrance it seemed to ring like a dulcimer on the frozen air.

How could his host, so mysterious, so kind, deny Beauty her present?

Not now distant but close at hand, close as that mahogany front door, rose a mighty, furious roaring; the garden seemed to hold its breath in apprehension. But still, because he loved his daughter, Beauty's father stole the rose.

At that, every window of the house blazed with furious light and a fugal baying, as of a pride of lions, introduced his host.

There is always a dignity about great bulk, an assertiveness, a quality of being more *there* than most of us are. The being who now confronted Beauty's father seemed to him, in his confusion, vaster than the house he owned, ponderous yet swift, and the moonlight glittered on his great, mazy head of hair, on the eyes green as agate, on the golden hairs of the great paws that grasped his shoulders so that their claws pierced the sheepskin as he shook him like an angry child shakes a doll.

This leonine apparition shook Beauty's father until his teeth rattled and then dropped him sprawling on his knees while the spaniel, darting from the open door, danced round them, yapping distractedly, like a lady at whose dinner party blows have been exchanged.

'My good fellow –' stammered Beauty's father; but the only response was a renewed roar.

'Good fellow? I am no good fellow! I am the Beast, and you must call me Beast, while I call you, Thief!'

'Forgive me for robbing your garden, Beast!'

Head of a lion; mane and mighty paws of a lion; he reared on his hind legs like an angry lion yet wore a smoking jacket of dull red brocade and was the owner of that lovely house and the low hills that cupped it.

'It was for my daughter,' said Beauty's father. 'All she wanted, in the whole world, was one white, perfect rose.'

The Beast rudely snatched the photograph her father drew from his wallet and inspected it, first brusquely, then with a strange kind of wonder, almost the dawning of surmise. The camera had captured a certain look she had, sometimes, of absolute sweetness and absolute gravity, as if her eyes might pierce appearances and see your soul. When he handed the picture back, the Beast took good care not to scratch the surface with his claws.

'Take her the rose, then, but bring her to dinner,' he growled; and what else was there to be done?

Although her father had told her of the nature of the one who waited for her, she could not control an instinctual shudder of fear when she saw him, for a lion is a lion and a man is a man and, though lions are more beautiful by far than we are, yet they belong to a different order of beauty and, besides, they have no respect for us: why should they? Yet wild things have a far more rational fear of us than is ours of them, and some kind of sadness in his agate eyes, that looked almost blind, as if sick of sight, moved her heart.

He sat, impassive as a figurehead, at the top of the table; the dining room was Queen Anne, tapestried, a gem. Apart from an aromatic soup kept hot over a spirit lamp, the food, though exquisite, was cold – a cold bird, a cold soufflé, cheese. He asked her father to serve them from a buffet and, himself, ate nothing. He grudgingly admitted what she had already guessed, that he disliked the presence of servants because, she thought, a constant human presence would remind him too bitterly of his otherness, but the spaniel sat at his feet throughout the meal, jumping up from time to time to see that everything was in order.

How strange he was. She found his bewildering difference from herself almost intolerable; its presence choked her. There seemed a heavy, soundless pressure upon her in his house, as if it lay under water, and when she saw the great paws lying on the arm of his chair, she thought: they are the death of any tender herbivore. And such a one she felt herself to be, Miss Lamb, spotless, sacrificial.

Yet she stayed, and smiled, because her father wanted her to do so; and when the Beast told her how he would aid her father's appeal against the judgement, she smiled with both her mouth and her eyes. But when, as they sipped their brandy, the Beast, in the diffuse, rumbling purr with which he conversed, suggested, with a hint of shyness, of fear of refusal, that she should stay here, with him, in comfort, while her father returned to London to take up the legal cudgels again, she forced a smile. For she knew with a pang of dread, as soon as he spoke, that it would be so and her visit to the Beast must be, on some magically reciprocal scale, the price of her father's good fortune.

Do not think she had no will of her own; only, she was possessed by a sense of obligation to an unusual degree and, besides, she would gladly have gone to the ends of the earth for her father, whom she loved dearly.

Her bedroom contained a marvellous glass bed; she had a bathroom, with towels thick as fleece and vials of suave unguents; and a little parlour of her own, the walls of which were covered with an antique paper of birds of paradise and Chinamen, where there were precious books and pictures and the flowers grown by invisible gardeners in the Beast's hothouses. Next morning, her father kissed her and drove away with a renewed hope about him that made her glad, but, all the same, she longed for the shabby home of their poverty. The unaccustomed luxury about her she found poignant, because it gave no pleasure to its possessor and himself she did not see all day as if, curious reversal, she frightened him, although the spaniel came and sat with her, to keep her company. Today, the spaniel wore a neat choker of turquoises.

Who prepared her meals? Loneliness of the Beast; all the time she stayed there, she saw no evidence of another human presence but the trays of food that arrived on a dumb waiter inside a mahogany cupboard in her parlour. Dinner was eggs Benedict and grilled veal; she ate it as she browsed in a book she had found in the rosewood revolving bookcase, a collection of courtly and elegant French fairy tales about white cats who were transformed princesses and fairies who were birds. Then she pulled a sprig of muscat grapes from a fat bunch for her dessert and found herself yawning; she discovered she was bored. At that, the spaniel took hold of her skirt with its velvet mouth and gave it a firm but gentle tug. She allowed the dog to trot before her to the study in which her father had been entertained and there, to her well-disguised dismay, she found her host, seated beside the fire with a tray of coffee at his elbow from which she must pour.

The voice that seemed to issue from a cave full of echoes, his dark, soft rumbling growl; after her day of pastel-coloured idleness, how could she converse with the possessor of a voice that seemed an instrument created to inspire the terror that the chords of great organs bring? Fascinated, almost awed, she watched the firelight play on the gold fringes of his mane; he was irradiated, as if with a kind of halo, and she thought of the first great beast of the Apocalypse, the winged lion with his paw upon the Gospel, Saint Mark. Small talk turned to dust in her mouth; small talk had never, at the best of times, been Beauty's forte, and she had little practice at it.

But he, hesitantly, as if he himself were in awe of a young girl who looked as if she had been carved out of a single pearl, asked after her father's law case; and her dead mother; and how they, who had been so rich, had come to be so poor. He forced himself to master his shyness, which was that of a wild creature, and so she contrived to master her own – to such effect that soon she was chattering away to him as if she had known him all her life. When the little cupid in the gilt clock on the mantelpiece struck its miniature tambourine, she was astonished to discover it did so twelve times.

'So late! You will want to sleep,' he said.

At that, they both fell silent, as if these strange companions were suddenly overcome with embarrassment to find themselves together, alone, in that room in the depths of the winter's night. As she was about to rise, he flung himself at her feet and buried his head in her lap. She stayed stock-still, transfixed; she felt his hot breath on her fingers, the stiff bristles of his muzzle grazing her skin, the rough lapping of his tongue and then, with a flood of compassion, understood: all he is doing is kissing my hands.

He drew back his head and gazed at her with his green, inscrutable eyes, in which she saw her face repeated twice, as small as if it were in bud. Then, without another word, he sprang from the room and she saw, with an indescribable shock, he went on all fours.

Next day, all day, the hills on which the snow still settled echoed with the Beast's rumbling roar: has master gone a-hunting? Beauty asked the spaniel. But the spaniel growled, almost bad-temperedly, as if to say, that she would not have answered, even if she could have.

Beauty would pass the day in her suite reading or, perhaps, doing a little embroidery; a box of coloured silks and a frame had been provided for her. Or, well wrapped up, she wandered in the walled garden, among the leafless roses, with the spaniel at her heels, and did a little raking and rearranging. An idle, restful time; a holiday. The enchantment of that bright, sad, pretty place enveloped her and she found that, against all her expectations, she was happy there. She no longer felt the slightest apprehension at her nightly interviews with the Beast. All the natural laws of the world were held in suspension, here, where an army of invisibles tenderly waited on her, and she would talk with the lion, under the patient chaperonage of the brown-eyed dog, on the nature of the moon and its borrowed light, about the stars and the substances of which they were made, about the variable transformations of the weather. Yet still his strangeness made her shiver; and when he helplessly fell before her to kiss her hands, as he did every

47

night when they parted, she would retreat nervously into her skin, flinching at his touch.

The telephone shrilled; for her. Her father. Such news!

The Beast sunk his great head on to his paws. You will come back to me? It will be lonely here, without you.

She was moved almost to tears that he should care for her so. It was in her heart to drop a kiss upon his shaggy mane but, though she stretched out her hand towards him, she could not bring herself to touch him of her own free will, he was so different from herself. But, yes, she said; I will come back. Soon, before the winter is over. Then the taxi came and took her away.

You are never at the mercy of the elements in London, where the huddled warmth of humanity melts the snow before it has time to settle; and her father was as good as rich again, since his hirsute friend's lawyers had the business so well in hand that his credit brought them nothing but the best. A resplendent hotel; the opera, theatres; a whole new wardrobe for his darling, so she could step out on his arm to parties, to receptions, to restaurants, and life was as she had never known it, for her father had ruined himself before her birth killed her mother.

Although the Beast was the source of this new-found prosperity and they talked of him often, now that they were so far away from the timeless spell of his house it seemed to possess the radiant and finite quality of dream and the Beast himself, so monstrous, so benign, some kind of spirit of good fortune who had smiled on them and let them go. She sent him flowers, white roses in return for the ones he had given her; and when she left the florist, she experienced a sudden sense of perfect freedom, as if she had just escaped from an unknown danger, had been grazed by the possibility of some change but, finally, left intact. Yet, with this exhilaration, a desolating emptiness. But her father was waiting for her at the hotel; they had planned a delicious expedition to buy her furs and she was as eager for the treat as any girl might be.

Since the flowers in the shop were the same all the year round, nothing in the window could tell her that winter had almost gone.

Returning late from supper after the theatre, she took off her earrings in front of the mirror; Beauty. She smiled at herself with satisfaction. She was learning, at the end of her adolescence, how to be a spoiled child and that pearly skin of hers was plumping out, a little, with high living and compliments. A certain inwardness was beginning to transform the lines around her mouth, those signatures of the personality, and her sweetness and her gravity could sometimes turn a mite petulant when things went not quite as she wanted them to go. You could not have said that her freshness was fading but she smiled at herself in mirrors a little too often, these days, and the face that smiled back was not quite the one she had seen contained in the Beast's agate eyes. Her face was acquiring, instead of beauty, a lacquer of the invincible prettiness that characterizes certain pampered, exquisite, expensive cats.

The soft wind of spring breathed in from the near-by park through the open windows; she did not know why it made her want to cry.

There was a sudden, urgent, scrabbling sound, as of claws, at her door.

Her trance before the mirror broke; all at once, she remembered everything perfectly. Spring was here and she had broken her promise. Now the Beast himself had come in pursuit of her! First, she was frightened of his anger; then, mysteriously joyful, she ran to open the door. But it was his liver and white spotted spaniel who hurled herself into the girl's arms in a flurry of little barks and gruff murmurings, of whimpering and relief.

Yet where was the well-brushed, jewelled dog who had sat beside her embroidery frame in the parlour with birds of paradise nodding on the walls? This one's fringed ears were matted with mud, her coat was dusty and snarled, she was thin as a dog that has walked a long way and, if she had not been a dog, she would have been in tears.

After that first, rapturous greeting, she did not wait for Beauty to order her food and water; she seized the chiffon hem of her evening dress, whimpered and tugged. Threw back her head, howled, then tugged and whimpered again.

There was a slow, late train that would take her to the station where she had left for London three months ago. Beauty scribbled a note for her father, threw a coat round her shoulders. Quickly, quickly, urged the spaniel soundlessly; and Beauty knew the Beast was dying.

In the thick dark before dawn, the station master roused a sleepy driver for her. Fast as you can.

It seemed December still possessed his garden. The ground was hard as iron, the skirts of the dark cypress moved on the chill wind with a mournful rustle and there were no green shoots on the roses as if, this year, they would not bloom. And not one light in any of the windows, only, in the topmost attic, the faintest smear of radiance on a pane, the thin ghost of a light on the verge of extinction.

The spaniel had slept a little, in her arms, for the poor thing was exhausted. But now her grieving agitation fed Beauty's urgency and, as the girl pushed open the front door, she saw, with a thrust of conscience, how the golden door knocker was thickly muffled in black crêpe.

The door did not open silently, as before, but with a doleful groaning of the hinges and, this time, on to perfect darkness. Beauty clicked her gold cigarette lighter; the tapers in the chandelier had drowned in their own wax and the prisms were wreathed with drifting arabesques of cobwebs. The flowers in the glass jars were dead, as if nobody had had the heart to replace them after she was gone. Dust, everywhere; and it was cold. There was an air of exhaustion, of despair in the house and, worse, a kind of physical disillusion, as if its glamour had been sustained by a cheap conjuring trick and now the conjurer, having failed to pull the crowds, had departed to try his luck elsewhere.

Beauty found a candle to light her way and followed the faithful spaniel up the staircase, past the study, past her suite, through a house echoing with desertion up a little back staircase dedicated to mice and spiders, stumbling, ripping the hem of her dress in her haste.

What a modest bedroom! An attic, with a sloping roof, they might have given the chambermaid if the Beast had employed staff. A night light on the mantelpiece, no curtains at the windows, no carpet on the floor and a narrow, iron bedstead on which he lay, sadly diminished, his bulk scarcely disturbing the faded patchwork quilt, his mane a greyish rat's nest and his eyes closed. On the stick-backed chair where his clothes had been thrown, the roses she had sent him were thrust into the jug from the washstand but they were all dead.

The spaniel jumped up on the bed and burrowed her way under the scanty covers, softly keening.

'Oh, Beast,' said Beauty. 'I have come home.'

His eyelids flickered. How was it she had never noticed before that his agate eyes were equipped with lids, like those of a man? Was it because she had only looked at her own face, reflected there?

'I'm dying, Beauty,' he said in a cracked whisper of his former purr. 'Since you left me, I have been sick. I could not go hunting, I found I had not the stomach to kill the gentle beasts, I could not eat. I am sick and I must die; but I shall die happy because you have come to say good-bye to me.'

She flung herself upon him, so that the iron bedstead groaned, and covered his poor paws with her kisses.

'Don't die, Beast! If you'll have me, I'll never leave you.'

When her lips touched the meat-hook claws, they drew back into their pads and she saw how he had always kept his fists clenched but now, painfully, tentatively, at last began to stretch his fingers. Her tears fell on his face like snow and, under their soft transformation, the bones showed through the pelt, the flesh through the wide, tawny brow. And then it was no longer a lion in her arms but a man, a man with an unkempt mane of hair and, how strange, a broken nose, such as the noses of retired boxers, that gave him a distant, heroic resemblance to the handsomest of all the beasts.

'Do you know,' said Mr Lyon, 'I think I might be able to manage a little breakfast today, Beauty, if you would eat something with me.'

Mr and Mrs Lyon walk in the garden; the old spaniel drowses on the grass, in a drift of fallen petals.

The Tiger's Bride

My father lost me to The Beast at cards.

There's a special madness strikes travellers from the North when they reach the lovely land where the lemon trees grow. We come from countries of cold weather; at home, we are at war with nature but here, ah! you think you've come to the blessed plot where the lion lies down with the lamb. Everything flowers; no harsh wind stirs the voluptuous air. The sun spills fruit for you. And the deathly, sensual lethargy of the sweet South infects the starved brain; it gasps: 'Luxury! more luxury!' But then the snow comes, you cannot escape it, it followed us from Russia as if it ran behind our carriage, and in this dark, bitter city has caught up with us at last, flocking against the windowpanes to mock my father's expectations of perpetual pleasure as the veins in his forehead stand out and throb, his hands shake as he deals the Devil's picture books.

The candles dropped hot, acrid gouts of wax on my bare shoulders. I watched with the furious cynicism peculiar to women whom circumstances force mutely to witness folly, while my father, fired in his desperation by more and yet more draughts of the firewater they call 'grappa', rids himself of the last scraps of my inheritance. When we left Russia, we owned black earth, blue forest with bear and wild boar, serfs, cornfields, farmyards, my beloved horses, white nights of cool summer, the fireworks of the northern lights. What a burden all those possessions must have been to him, because he laughs as if with glee as he beggars himself; he is in such a passion to donate all to The Beast.

Everyone who comes to this city must play a hand with the *grand seigneur*; few come. They did not warn us at Milan, or, if they did, we did not understand them – my limping Italian, the bewildering dialect of the region. Indeed, I myself spoke up in favour of this remote, provincial place, out of fashion two hundred years, because, oh irony, it boasted no casino. I did not know that the price of a stay in its Decembral solitude was a game with Milord.

The hour was late. The chill damp of this place creeps into the stones, into your bones, into the spongy pith of the lungs; it insinuated itself with a shiver into our parlour, where Milord came to play in the privacy essential to him. Who could refuse the invitation his valet brought to our lodging? Not my profligate father, certainly; the mirror above the table gave me back his frenzy, my impassivity, the withering candles, the emptying bottles, the coloured tide of the cards as they rose and fell, the still mask that concealed all the features of The Beast but for the yellow eyes that strayed, now and then, from his unfurled hand towards myself.

'La Bestia!' said our landlady, gingerly fingering an envelope with his huge crest of a tiger rampant on it, something of fear, something of wonder in her face. And I could not ask her why they called the master of the place, 'La Bestia' – was it to do with that heraldic signature? – because her tongue was so thickened by the phlegmy, bronchitic speech of the region I scarcely managed to make out a thing she said except, when she saw me: 'Che bella!'

Since I could toddle, always the pretty one, with my glossy, nut-brown curls, my rosy cheeks. And born on Christmas Day – her 'Christmas rose', my English nurse called me. The peasants said: 'The living image of her mother,' crossing themselves out of respect for the dead. My mother did not blossom long; bartered for her dowry to such a feckless sprig of the Russian nobility that she soon died of his gaming, his whoring, his agonizing repentances. And The Beast gave me the rose from his own impeccable if outmoded buttonhole when he arrived, the valet brushing the snow off his black cloak. This white rose, unnatural, out of season, that now my nervous fingers ripped, petal by petal, apart as my father magnificently concluded the career he had made of catastrophe.

This is a melancholy, introspective region; a sunless, featureless landscape, the sullen river sweating fog, the shorn, hunkering willows. And a cruel city; the sombre piazza, a place uniquely suited to public executions, under the beetling shadow of that malign barn of a church. They used to hang condemned men in cages from the city walls; unkindness comes naturally to them, their eyes are set too close together, they have thin lips. Poor food, pasta soaked in oil, boiled beef with sauce of bitter herbs. A funereal hush about the place, the inhabitants huddled up against the cold so you can hardly see their faces. And they lie to you and cheat you, innkeepers, coachmen, everybody. God, how they fleeced us!

The treacherous South, where you think there is no winter but forget you take it with you.

My senses were increasingly troubled by the fuddling perfume of Milord, far too potent a reek of purplish civet at such close quarters in so small a room. He must bathe himself in scent, soak his shirts and underlinen in it; what can he smell of, that needs so much camouflage?

I never saw a man so big look so two-dimensional, in spite of the quaint elegance of The Beast, in the old-fashioned tailcoat that might, from its looks, have been bought in those distant years before he imposed seclusion on himself; he does not feel he need keep up with the times. There is a crude clumsiness about his outlines, that are on the ungainly, giant side; and he has an odd air of self-imposed restraint, as if fighting a battle with himself to remain upright when he would far rather drop down on all fours. He throws our human aspirations to the godlike sadly awry, poor fellow; only from a distance would you think The Beast not much different from any other man, although he wears a mask with a man's face painted most beautifully on it. Oh, yes, a beautiful face; but one with too much formal symmetry of feature to be entirely human: one profile of his mask is the mirror image of the other, too perfect, uncanny. He wears a wig, too, false hair tied at the nape with a bow, a wig of the kind you see in old-fashioned portraits. A chaste silk stock stuck with a pearl hides his throat. And gloves of blond kid that are yet so huge and clumsy they do not seem to cover hands.

He is a carnival figure made of papier mâché and crêpe hair; and yet he has the Devil's knack at cards.

His masked voice echoes as from a great distance as he stoops over his hand and he has such a growling impediment in his speech that only his valet, who understands him, can interpret for him, as if his master were the clumsy doll and he the ventriloquist.

The wick slumped in the eroded wax, the candles guttered. By the time my rose had lost all its petals, my father, too, was left with nothing.

'Except the girl.'

Gambling is a sickness. My father said he loved me yet he staked his daughter on a hand of cards. He fanned them out; in the mirror, I saw wild hope light up his eyes. His collar was unfastened, his rumpled hair stood up on end, he had the anguish of a man in the last stages of debauchery. The draughts came out of the old walls and bit me, I was colder than I'd ever been in Russia, when nights are coldest there.

A queen, a king, an ace. I saw them in the mirror. Oh, I know he thought he could not lose me; besides, back with me would come all he had lost, the unravelled fortunes of our family at one blow restored. And would he not win, as well, The Beast's hereditary palazzo outside the city; his immense revenues; his lands around the river; his rents, his treasure chest, his Mantegnas, his Giulio Romanos, his Cellini salt-cellars, his titles . . . the very city itself.

You must not think my father valued me at less than a king's ransom; but, at *no more* than a king's ransom.

It was cold as hell in the parlour. And it seemed to me, child of the severe North, that it was not my flesh but, truly, my father's soul that was in peril.

My father, of course, believed in miracles; what gambler does not? In pursuit of just such a miracle as this, had we not travelled from the land of bears and shooting stars?

So we teetered on the brink.

The Beast bayed; laid down all three remaining aces.

The indifferent servants now glided smoothly forward as on wheels to douse the candles one by one. To look at them you would think that nothing of any moment had occurred. They yawned a little resentfully; it was almost morning, we had kept them out of bed. The Beast's man brought his cloak. My father sat amongst these preparations for departure, staring on at the betrayal of his cards upon the table.

The Beast's man informed me crisply that he, the valet, would call for me and my bags tomorrow, at ten, and conduct me forthwith to The Beast's palazzo. Capisco? So shocked was I that I scarcely did 'capisco'; he repeated my orders patiently, he was a strange, thin, quick little man who walked with an irregular, jolting rhythm upon splayed feet in curious, wedge-shaped shoes.

Where my father had been red as fire, now he was white as the snow that caked the window-pane. His eyes swam; soon he would cry.

' "Like the base Indian," ' he said; he loved rhetoric. ' "One whose hand,/Like the base Indian, threw a pearl away/Richer than all his tribe . . ." I have lost my pearl, my pearl beyond price.'

At that, The Beast made a sudden, dreadful noise, halfway between a growl and a roar; the candles flared. The quick valet, the prim hypocrite, interpreted unblinking: 'My master says: If you are so careless of your treasures, you should expect them to be taken from you.'

He gave us the bow and smile his master could not offer us and they departed.

I watched the snow until, just before dawn, it stopped falling; a hard frost settled, next morning there was a light like iron.

The Beast's carriage, of an elegant if antique design, was black as a hearse and it was drawn by a dashing black gelding who blew smoke from his nostrils and stamped upon the packed snow with enough sprightly appearance of life to give me some hope that not all the world was locked in ice, as I was. I had always held a little towards Gulliver's opinion, that horses are better than we are, and, that day, I would have been glad to depart with him to the kingdom of horses, if I'd been given the chance.

The valet sat up on the box in a natty black and gold livery, clasping, of all things, a bunch of his master's damned white roses as if a gift of flowers would reconcile a woman to any humiliation. He sprang down with preternatural agility to place them ceremoniously in my reluctant hand. My tear-beslobbered father wants a rose to show that I forgive him. When I break off a stem, I prick my finger and so he gets his rose all smeared with blood.

The valet crouched at my feet to tuck the rugs about me with a strange kind of unflattering obsequiousness yet he forgot his station sufficiently to scratch busily beneath his white periwig with an over-supple index finger as he offered me what my old nurse would have called an 'old-fashioned look', ironic, sly, a smidgen of disdain in it. And pity? No pity. His eyes were moist and brown, his face seamed with the innocent cunning of an ancient baby. He had an irritating habit of chattering to himself under his breath all the time as he packed up his master's winnings. I drew the curtains to conceal the sight of my father's farewell; my spite was sharp as broken glass.

Lost to The Beast! And what, I wondered, might be the exact nature of his 'beastliness'? My English nurse once told me about a tiger-man she saw in London, when she was a little girl, to scare me into good behaviour, for I was a wild wee thing and she could not tame me into submission with a frown or the bribe of a spoonful of jam. If you don't stop plaguing the nursemaids, my beauty, the tiger-man will come and take you away. They'd brought him from Sumatra, in the Indies, she said; his hinder parts were all hairy and only from the head downwards did he resemble a man.

And yet The Beast goes always masked; it cannot be his face that looks like mine.

But the tiger-man, in spite of his hairiness, could take a glass of ale in his hand like a good Christian and drink it down. Had she not seen him do so, at the sign of The George, by the steps of Upper Moor Fields when she was just as high as me and lisped and toddled, too. Then she would sigh for London, across the North Sea of the lapse of years. But, if this young lady was not a good little girl and did not eat her boiled beetroot, then the tiger-man would put on his big black travelling cloak lined with fur, just like your daddy's, and hire the Erl-King's galloper of wind and ride through the night straight to the nursery and –

Yes, my beauty! GOBBLE YOU UP!

How I'd squeal in delighted terror, half believing her, half knowing that she teased me. And there were things I knew that I must not tell her. In our lost farmyard, where the giggling nursemaids initiated me into the mysteries of what the bull did to the cows, I heard about the waggoner's daughter. Hush, hush, don't let on to your nursie we said so; the waggoner's lass, hare-lipped, squint-eyed, ugly as sin, who would have taken her? Yet, to her shame, her belly swelled amid the cruel mockery of the ostlers and her son was born of a bear, they whispered. Born with a full pelt and teeth; that proved it. But, when he grew up, he was a good shepherd, although he never married, lived in a hut outside the village and could make the wind blow any way he wanted to besides being able to tell which eggs would become cocks, which hens.

The wondering peasants once brought my father a skull with horns four inches long on either side of it and would not go back to the field where their poor plough disturbed it until the priest went with them; for this skull had the jaw-bone of a *man*, had it not?

Old wives' tales, nursery fears! I knew well enough the reason for the trepidation I cosily titillated with superstitious marvels of my childhood on the day my childhood ended. For now my own skin was my sole capital in the world and today I'd make my first investment

We had left the city far behind us and were now traversing a wide, flat dish of snow where the mutilated stumps of the willows flourished their ciliate heads athwart frozen ditches; mist diminished the horizon, brought down the sky until it seemed no more than a few inches above us. As far as eye could see, not one thing living. How starveling, how bereft the dead season of this spurious Eden in which all the fruit was blighted by cold! And my frail roses, already faded. I opened the carriage door and tossed the defunct bouquet into the rucked, frost-stiff mud of the road. Suddenly a sharp, freezing wind arose and pelted my face with a dry rice of powdered snow. The mist lifted sufficiently to reveal before me an acreage of half-derelict façades of sheer red brick, the vast man-trap, the megalomaniac citadel of his palazzo.

It was a world in itself but a dead one, a burned-out planet. I saw The Beast bought solitude, not luxury, with his money.

The little black horse trotted smartly through the figured bronze doors that stood open to the weather like those of a barn and the valet handed me out of the carriage on to the scarred tiles of the great hall itself, into the odorous warmth of a stable, sweet with hay, acrid with horse dung. An equine chorus of neighings and soft drummings of hooves broke out beneath the tall roof, where the beams were scabbed with last summer's swallows' nests; a dozen gracile muzzles lifted from their mangers and turned towards us, ears erect. The Beast had given his horses the use of the dining room. The walls were painted, aptly enough, with a fresco of horses, dogs and men in a wood where fruit and blossom grew on the bough together.

The valet tweaked politely at my sleeve. Milord is waiting.

Gaping doors and broken windows let the wind in everywhere. We mounted one staircase after another, our feet clopping on the marble. Through archways and open doors, I glimpsed suites of vaulted chambers opening one out of another like systems of Chinese boxes into the infinite complexity of the innards of the place. He and I and the wind were the only things stirring; and all the furniture was under dust sheets, the chandeliers bundled up in cloth, pictures taken from their hooks and propped with their faces to the walls as if their master could not bear to look at them. The palace was dismantled, as if its owner were about to move house or had never properly moved in; The Beast had chosen to live in an uninhabited place.

The valet darted me a reassuring glance from his brown, eloquent eyes, yet a glance with so much queer superciliousness in it that it did not comfort me, and went bounding ahead of me on his bandy legs, softly chattering to himself. I held my head high and followed him; but, for all my pride, my heart was heavy.

Milord has his eyrie high above the house, a small, stifling, darkened room; he keeps his shutters locked at noon. I was out of breath by the time we reached it and returned to him the silence with which he greeted me. I will not smile. He cannot smile.

In his rarely disturbed privacy, The Beast wears a garment of Ottoman design, a loose, dull purple gown with gold embroidery round the neck that falls from his shoulders to conceal his feet. The feet of the chair he sits in are handsomely clawed. He hides his hands in his ample sleeves. The artificial masterpiece of his face appals me. A small fire in a small grate. A rushing wind rattles the shutters.

The valet coughed. To him fell the delicate task of transmitting to me his master's wishes.

'My master –'

A stick fell in the grate. It made a mighty clatter in that dreadful silence; the valet started; lost his place in his speech, began again.

'My master has but one desire.'

The thick, rich, wild scent with which Milord had soaked himself the previous evening hangs all about us, ascends in cursive blue from the smoke of a precious Chinese pot.

'He wishes only –'

Now, in the face of my impassivity, the valet twittered, his ironic composure gone, for the desire of a master, however trivial, may yet sound unbearably insolent in the mouth of a servant and his role of go-between clearly caused him a good deal of embarrassment. He gulped; he swallowed, at last contrived to unleash an unpunctuated flood.

'My master's sole desire is to see the pretty young lady unclothed nude without her dress and that only for the one time after which she will be returned to her father undamaged with bankers' orders for the sum which he lost to my master at cards and also a number of fine presents such as furs, jewels and horses –'

I remained standing. During this interview, my eyes were level with those inside the mask that now evaded mine as if, to his credit, he was ashamed of his own request even as his mouthpiece made it for him. Agitato, molto agitato, the valet wrung his white-gloved hands.

'Desnuda –'

I could scarcely believe my ears. I let out a raucous guffaw; no young lady laughs like that! my old nurse used to remonstrate. But I did. And do. At the clamour of my heartless mirth, the valet danced backwards with perturbation, palpitating his fingers as if attempting to wrench them off, expostulating, wordlessly pleading. I felt that I owed it to him to make my reply in as exquisite a Tuscan as I could master.

'You may put me in a windowless room, sir, and I promise you I will pull my skirt up to my waist, ready for you. But there must be a sheet over my face, to hide it; though the sheet must be laid over me so lightly that it will not choke me. So I shall be covered completely from the waist upwards, and no lights. There you can visit me once, sir, and only the once. After that I must be driven directly to the city and deposited in the public square, in front of the church. If you wish to give me money, then I should be pleased to receive it. But I must stress that you should give me only the same amount of money that you would give to any other woman in such circumstances. However, if you choose not to give me a present, then that is your right.'

How pleased I was to see I struck The Beast to the heart! For, after a baker's dozen heartbeats, one single tear swelled, glittering, at the corner of the masked eye. A tear! A tear, I hoped, of shame. The tear trembled for a moment on an edge of painted bone, then tumbled down the painted cheek to fall, with an abrupt tinkle, on the tiled floor.

The valet, ticking and clucking to himself, hastily ushered me out of the room. A mauve cloud of his master's perfume billowed out into the chill corridor with us and dissipated itself on the spinning winds.

A cell had been prepared for me, a veritable cell, windowless, airless, lightless, in the viscera of the palace. The valet lit a lamp for me; a narrow bed, a dark cupboard with fruit and flowers carved on it bulked out of the gloom.

'I shall twist a noose out of my bed linen and hang myself with it,' I said.

'Oh, no,' said the valet, fixing upon me wide and suddenly melancholy eyes. 'Oh, no, you will not. You are a woman of honour.'

And what was *he* doing in my bedroom, this jigging caricature of a man? Was he to be my warder until I submitted to The Beast's whim or he to mine? Am I in such reduced circumstances that I may not have a lady's maid? As if in reply to my unspoken demand, the valet clapped his hands.

'To assuage your loneliness, madame . . .'

A knocking and clattering behind the door of the cupboard; the door swings open and out glides a soubrette from an operetta, with glossy, nut-brown curls, rosy cheeks, blue, rolling eyes; it takes me a moment to recognize her, in her little cap, her white stockings, her frilled petticoats. She carries a looking glass in one hand and a powder puff in the other and there is a musical box where her heart should be; she tinkles as she rolls towards me on her tiny wheels.

'Nothing human lives here,' said the valet.

My maid halted, bowed; from a split seam at the side of her bodice protrudes the handle of a key. She is a marvellous machine, the most delicately balanced system of cords and pulleys in the world.

'We have dispensed with servants,' the valet said. 'We surround ourselves, instead, for utility and pleasure, with simulacra and find it no less convenient than do most gentlemen.'

This clockwork twin of mine halted before me, her bowels churning out a settecento minuet, and offered me the bold carnation of her smile. Click, click – she raises her arm and busily dusts my cheeks with pink, powdered chalk that makes me cough; then thrusts towards me her little mirror.

I saw within it not my own face but that of my father, as if I had put on his face when I arrived at The Beast's palace as the discharge of his debt. What, you self-deluding fool, are you crying still? And drunk, too. He tossed back his grappa and hurled the tumbler away.

Seeing my astonished fright, the valet took the mirror away from me, breathed on it, polished it with the ham of his gloved fist, handed it back to me. Now all I saw was myself, haggard from a sleepless night, pale enough to need my maid's supply of rouge.

I heard the key turn in the heavy door and the valet's footsteps patter down the stone passage. Meanwhile, my double continued to powder the air, emitting her jangling tune but, as it turned out, she was not inexhaustible; soon she was powdering more and yet more languorously, her metal heart slowed in imitation of fatigue, her musical box ran down until the notes separated themselves out of the tune and plopped like single raindrops and, as if sleep had overtaken her, at last she moved no longer. As she succumbed to sleep, I had no option but to do so, too. I dropped on that narrow bed as if felled.

Time passed but I do not know how much; then the valet woke me with rolls and honey. I gestured the tray away but he set it down firmly beside the lamp and took from it a little shagreen box, which he offered to me.

I turned away my head.

'Oh, my lady!' Such hurt cracked his high-pitched voice! He dextrously unfastened the gold clasp; on a bed of crimson velvet lay a single diamond earring, perfect as a tear.

I snapped the box shut and tossed it into a corner. This sudden, sharp movement must have disturbed the mechanism of the doll; she jerked her arm almost as if to reprimand me, letting out a rippling fart of gavotte. Then was still again.

'Very well,' said the valet, put out. And indicated it was time for me to visit my host again. He did not let me wash or comb my hair. There was so little natural light in the interior of the palace that I could not tell whether it was day or night.

You would not think The Beast had budged an inch since I last saw him; he sat in his huge chair, with his hands in his sleeves, and the heavy air never moved. I might have slept an hour, a night, or a month, but his sculptured calm, the stifling air remained just as it had been. The incense rose from the pot, still traced the same signature on the air. The same fire burned.

Take off my clothes for you, like a ballet girl? Is that all you want of me?

'The sight of a young lady's skin that no man has seen before –' stammered the valet.

I wished I'd rolled in the hay with every lad on my father's farm, to disqualify myself from this humiliating bargain. That he should want so little was the reason why I could not give it; I did not need to speak for The Beast to understand me.

A tear came from his other eye. And then he moved; he buried his cardboard carnival head with its ribboned weight of false hair in, I would say, his arms; he withdrew his, I might say, hands from his sleeves and I saw his furred pads, his excoriating claws.

The dropped tear caught upon his fur and shone. And in my room for hours I hear those paws pad back and forth outside my door.

When the valet arrived again with his silver salver, I had a pair of diamond earrings of the finest water in the world; I threw the other into the corner where the first one lay. The valet twittered with aggrieved regret but did not offer to lead me to The Beast again. Instead, he smiled ingratiatingly and confided: 'My master, he say: invite the young lady to go riding.'

'What's this?'

He briskly mimicked the action of a gallop and, to my amazement, tunelessly croaked: 'Tantivy! tantivy! a-hunting we will go!'

'I'll run away, I'll ride to the city.'

'Oh, no,' he said. 'Are you not a woman of honour?'

He clapped his hands and my maidservant clicked and jangled into the imitation of life. She rolled towards the cupboard where she had come from and reached inside it to fetch out over her synthetic arm my riding habit. Of all things. My very own riding habit, that I'd left behind me in a trunk in a loft in that country house outside Petersburg that we'd lost long ago, before, even, we set out on this wild pilgrimage to the cruel South. Either the very riding habit my old nurse had sewn for me or else a copy of it perfect to the lost button on the right sleeve, the ripped hem held up with a pin. I turned the worn cloth about in my hands, looking for a clue. The wind that sprinted through the palace made the door tremble in its frame; had the north wind blown my garments across Europe to me? At home, the bear's son directed the winds at his pleasure; what democracy of magic held this palace and the fir forest in common? Or, should I be prepared to accept it as proof of the axiom my father had drummed into me: that, if you have enough money, anything is possible?

'Tantivy,' suggested the now twinkling valet, evidently charmed at the pleasure mixed with my bewilderment. The clockwork maid held my jacket out to me and I allowed myself to shrug into it as if reluctantly, although I was half mad to get out into the open air, away from this deathly palace, even in such company.

The doors of the hall let the bright day in; I saw that it was morning. Our horses, saddled and bridled, beasts in bondage, were waiting for us, striking sparks from the tiles with their impatient hooves while their stablemates lolled at ease among the straw, conversing with one another in the mute speech of horses. A pigeon or two, feathers puffed to keep out the cold, strutted about, pecking at ears of corn. The little black gelding who had brought me here greeted me with a ringing neigh that resonated inside the misty roof as in a sounding box and I knew he was meant for me to ride.

I always adored horses, noblest of creatures, such wounded sensitivity in their wise eyes, such rational restraint of energy at their high-strung hindquarters. I lirruped and hurrumphed to my shining black companion and he acknowledged my greeting with a kiss on the forehead from his soft lips. There was a little shaggy pony nuzzling away at the *trompe l'œil* foliage beneath the hooves of the painted horses on the wall, into whose saddle the valet sprang with a flourish as of the circus. Then The Beast, wrapped in a black fur-lined cloak, came to heave himself aloft a grave grey mare. No natural horseman he; he clung to her mane like a shipwrecked sailor to a spar.

Cold, that morning, yet dazzling with the sharp winter sunlight that wounds the retina. There was a scurrying wind about that seemed to go with us, as if the masked, immense one who did not speak carried it inside his cloak and let it out at his pleasure, for it stirred the horses' manes but did not lift the lowland mists.

A bereft landscape in the sad browns and sepias of winter lay all about us, the marshland drearily protracting itself towards the wide river. Those decapitated willows. Now and then, the swoop of a bird, its irreconcilable cry.

A profound sense of strangeness slowly began to possess me. I knew my two companions were not, in any way, as other men, the simian retainer and the master for whom he spoke, the one with clawed fore-paws who was in a plot with the witches who let the winds out of their knotted handkerchiefs up towards the Finnish border. I knew they lived according to a different logic than I had done until my father abandoned me to the wild beasts by his human carelessness. This knowledge gave me a certain fearfulness still; but, I would say, not much ... I was a young girl, a virgin, and therefore men denied me rationality just as they denied it to all those who were not exactly like themselves, in all their unreason. If I could see not one single soul in that wilderness of desolation all around me, then the six of us – mounts and riders, both – could boast amongst us not one soul, either, since all the best religions in the world state categorically that not beasts nor women were equipped with the flimsy, insubstantial things when the good Lord opened the gates of Eden and let Eve and her familiars tumble out. Understand, then, that though I would not say I privately engaged in metaphysical speculation as we rode through the reedy approaches to the river, I certainly meditated on the nature of my own state, how I had been bought and sold, passed from hand to hand. That clockwork girl who powdered my cheeks for me; had I not been allotted only the same kind of imitative life amongst men that the doll-maker had given her?

Yet, as to the true nature of the being of this clawed magus who rode his pale horse in a style that made me recall how Kublai Khan's leopards went out hunting on horseback, of that I had no notion.

We came to the bank of the river that was so wide we could not see across it, so still with winter that it scarcely seemed to flow. The horses lowered their heads to drink. The valet cleared his throat, about to speak; we were in a place of perfect privacy, beyond a brake of winter-bare rushes, a hedge of reeds.

'If you will not let him see you without your clothes –'

I involuntarily shook my head –

'– you must, then, prepare yourself for the sight of my master, naked.'

The river broke on the pebbles with a diminishing sigh. My composure deserted me; all at once I was on the brink of panic. I did not think that I could bear the sight of him, whatever he was. The mare raised her dripping muzzle and looked at me keenly, as if urging me. This river broke again at my feet. I was far from home.

'You,' said the valet, 'must.'

When I saw how scared he was I might refuse, I nodded.

The reed bowed down in a sudden snarl of wind that brought with it a gust of the heavy odour of his disguise. The valet held out his master's cloak to screen him from me as he removed the mask. The horses stirred.

The tiger will never lie down with the lamb; he acknowledges no pact that is not reciprocal. The lamb must learn to run with the tigers.

A great, feline, tawny shape whose pelt was barred with a savage geometry of bars the colour of burned wood. His domed, heavy head, so terrible he must hide it. How subtle the muscles, how profound the tread. The annihilating vehemence of his eyes, like twin suns.

I felt my breast ripped apart as if I suffered a marvellous wound.

The valet moved forward as if to cover up his master now the girl had acknowledged him, but I said: 'No.' The tiger sat still as a heraldic beast, in the pact he had made with his own ferocity to do me no harm. He was far larger than I could have imagined, from the poor, shabby things I'd seen once, in the Czar's menagerie at Petersburg, the golden fruit of their eyes dimming, withering in the far North of captivity. Nothing about him reminded me of humanity.

I therefore, shivering, now unfastened my jacket, to show him I would do him no harm. Yet I was clumsy and blushed a little, for no man had seen me naked and I was a proud girl. Pride it was, not shame, that thwarted my fingers so; and a certain trepidation lest this frail little article of human upholstery before him might not be, in itself, grand enough to satisfy his expectations of us, since those, for all I knew, might have grown infinite during the endless time he had been waiting. The wind clattered in the rushes, purled and eddied in the river.

I showed his grave silence my white skin, my red nipples, and the horses turned their heads to watch me, also, as if they, too, were courteously curious as to the fleshly nature of women. Then The Beast lowered his massive head; Enough! said the valet with a gesture. The wind died down, all was still again.

Then they went off together, the valet on his pony, the tiger running before him like a hound, and I walked along the river bank for a while. I felt I was at liberty for the first time in my life. Then the winter sun began to tarnish, a few flakes of snow drifted from the darkening sky and, when I returned to the horses, I found The Beast mounted again on his grey mare, cloaked and masked and once more, to all appearances, a man, while the valet had a fine catch of waterfowl dangling from his hand and the corpse of a young roebuck slung behind his saddle. I climbed up on the black gelding in silence and so we returned to the palace as the snow fell more and more heavily, obscuring the tracks that we had left behind us.

The valet did not return me to my cell but, instead, to an elegant, if old-fashioned boudoir with sofas of faded pink brocade, a jinn's treasury of Oriental carpets, tintinnabulation of cut-glass chandeliers. Candles in antlered holders struck rainbows from the prismatic hearts of my diamond earrings, that lay on my new dressing table at which my attentive maid stood ready with her powder puff and mirror. Intending to fix the ornaments in my ears, I took the looking glass from her hand, but it was in the midst of one of its magic fits again and I did not see my own face in it but that of my father; at first I thought he smiled at me. Then I saw he was smiling with pure gratification.

He sat, I saw, in the parlour of our lodgings, at the very table where he had lost me, but now he was busily engaged in counting out a tremendous pile of banknotes. My father's circumstances had changed already; well-shaven, neatly barbered, smart new clothes. A frosted glass of sparkling wine sat convenient to his hand beside an ice bucket. The Beast had clearly paid cash on the nail for his glimpse of my bosom, and paid up promptly, as if it had not been a sight I might have died of showing. Then I saw my father's trunks were packed, ready for departure. Could he so easily leave me here?

There was a note on the table with the money, in a fine hand. I could read it quite clearly. 'The young lady will arrive immediately.' Some harlot with whom he'd briskly negotiated a liaison on the strength of his spoils? Not at all. For, at that moment, the valet knocked at my door to announce that I might leave the palace at any time hereafter, and he bore over his arm a handsome sable cloak, my very own little gratuity, The Beast's morning gift, in which he proposed to pack me up and send me off.

When I looked at the mirror again, my father had disappeared and all I saw was a pale, hollow-eyed girl whom I scarcely recognized. The valet asked politely when he should prepare the carriage, as if he did not doubt that I would leave with my booty at the first opportunity while my maid, whose face was no longer the spit of my own, continued bonnily to beam. I will dress her in my own clothes, wind her up, send her back to perform the part of my father's daughter.

'Leave me alone,' I said to the valet.

65

He did not need to lock the door, now. I fixed the earrings in my ears. They were very heavy. Then I took off my riding habit, left it where it lay on the floor. But, when I got down to my shift, my arms dropped to my sides. I was unaccustomed to nakedness. I was so unused to my own skin that to take off all my clothes involved a kind of flaying. I thought The Beast had wanted a little thing compared with what I was prepared to give him; but it is not natural for humankind to go naked, not since first we hid our loins with fig leaves. He had demanded the abominable. I felt as much atrocious pain as if I was stripping off my own underpelt and the smiling girl stood poised in the oblivion of her balked simulation of life, watching me peel down to the cold, white meat of contract and, if she did not see me, then so much more like the market place, where the eyes that watch you take no account of your existence.

And it seemed my entire life, since I had left the North, had passed under the indifferent gaze of eyes like hers.

Then I was flinching stark, except for his irreproachable tears.

I huddled in the furs I must return to him, to keep me from the lacerating winds that raced along the corridors. I knew the way to his den without the valet to guide me.

No response to my tentative rap on his door.

Then the wind blew the valet whirling along the passage. He must have decided that, if one should go naked, then all should go naked; without his livery, he revealed himself, as I had suspected, a delicate creature, covered with silken moth-grey fur, brown fingers supple as leather, chocolate muzzle, the gentlest creature in the world. He gibbered a little to see my fine furs and jewels as if I were dressed up for the opera and, with a great deal of tender ceremony, removed the sables from my shoulders. The sables thereupon resolved themselves into a pack of black, squeaking rats that rattled immediately down the stairs on their hard little feet and were lost to sight.

The valet bowed me inside The Beast's room.

The purple dressing gown, the mask, the wig, were laid out on his chair; a glove was planted on each arm. The empty house of his appearance was ready for him but he had abandoned it. There was a reek of fur and piss; the incense pot lay broken in pieces on the floor. Half-burned sticks were scattered from the extinguished fire. A candle stuck by its own grease to the mantelpiece lit two narrow flames in the pupils of the tiger's eyes.

He was pacing backwards and forwards, backwards and forwards, the tip of his heavy tail twitching as he paced out the length and breadth of his imprisonment between the gnawed and bloody bones.

He will gobble you up.

Nursery fears made flesh and sinew; earliest and most archaic of fears, fear of devourment. The beast and his carnivorous bed of bone and I, white, shaking, raw, approaching him as if offering, in myself, the key to a peaceable kingdom in which his appetite need not be my extinction.

He went still as stone. He was far more frightened of me than I was of him.

I squatted on the wet straw and stretched out my hand. I was now within the field of force of his golden eyes. He growled at the back of his throat, lowered his head, sank on to his forepaws, snarled, showed me his red gullet, his yellow teeth. I never moved. He snuffed the air, as if to smell my fear; he could not.

Slowly, slowly he began to drag his heavy, gleaming weight across the floor towards me.

A tremendous throbbing, as of the engine that makes the earth turn, filled the little room; he had begun to purr.

The sweet thunder of this purr shook the old walls, made the shutters batter the windows until they burst apart and let in the white light of the snowy moon. Tiles came crashing down from the roof; I heard them fall into the courtyard far below. The reverberations of his purring rocked the foundations of the house, the walls began to dance. I thought: 'It will all fall, everything will disintegrate.'

He dragged himself closer and closer to me, until I felt the harsh velvet of his head against my hand, then a tongue, abrasive as sandpaper. 'He will lick the skin off me!'

And each stroke of his tongue ripped off skin after successive skin, all the skins of a life in the world, and left behind a nascent patina of shining hairs. My earrings turned back to water and trickled down my shoulders; I shrugged the drops off my beautiful fur.

Puss-in-Boots

Figaro here; Figaro, there, I tell you! Figaro upstairs, Figaro down-stairs and – oh, my goodness me, this little Figaro can slip into my lady's chamber smart as you like at any time whatsoever that he takes the fancy for, don't you know, he's a cat of the world, cosmopolitan, sophisticated; he can tell when a furry friend is the Missus' best company. For what lady in all the world could say 'no' to the passionate yet toujours discret advances of a fine marmalade cat? (Unless it be her eyes incontinently overflow at the slightest whiff of fur, which happened once, as you shall hear.)

A tom, sirs, a ginger tom and proud of it. Proud of his fine, white shirtfront that dazzles harmoniously against his orange and tangerine tessellations (oh! what a fiery suit of lights have I); proud of his bird-entrancing eye and more than military whiskers; proud, to a fault, some say, of his fine, musical voice. All the windows in the square fly open when I break into impromptu song at the spectacle of the moon above Bergamo. If the poor players in the square, the sullen rout of ragged trash that haunts the provinces, are rewarded with a hail of pennies when they set up their makeshift stage and start their raucous choruses, then how much more liberally do the citizens deluge me with pails of the freshest water, vegetables hardly spoiled and, occa-sionally, slippers, shoes and boots.

Do you see these fine, high, shining leather boots of mine? A young cavalry officer made me the tribute of, first, one; then, after I celebrate his generosity with a fresh obbligato, the moon no fuller than my heart – whoops! I nimbly spring aside – down comes the other. Their high heels will click like castanets when Puss takes his promenade upon the tiles, for my song recalls flamenco, all cats have a Spanish tinge although Puss himself elegantly lubricates his virile, muscular, native Bergamasque with French, since that is the only language in which you can purr.

'Merrrrrrrrrrrrci!'

Instanter I draw my new boots on over the natty white stockings that terminate my hinder legs. That young man, observing with curiosity by moonlight the use to which I put his footwear, calls out: 'Hey, Puss! Puss, there!'

'At your service, sir!'

'Up to my balcony, young Puss!'

He leans out, in his nightshirt, offering encouragement as I swing succinctly up the façade, forepaws on a curly cherub's pate, hindpaws on a stucco wreath, bring them up to meet your forepaws while, first paw forward, hup! on to the stone nymph's tit; left paw down a bit, the satyr's bum should do the trick. Nothing to it, once you know how, rococo's no problem. Acrobatics? Born to them; Puss can perform a back somersault whilst holding aloft a glass of vino in his right paw and *never spill a drop*.

But, to my shame, the famous death-defying triple somersault en plein air, that is, in middle air, that is, unsupported and without a safety net, I, Puss, have never yet attempted though often I have dashingly brought off the double tour, to the applause of all.

'You strike me as a cat of parts,' says this young man when I'm arrived at his window-sill. I made him a handsome genuflection, rump out, tail up, head down, to facilitate his friendly chuck under my chin; and, as involuntary free gift, my natural, my habitual smile.

For all cats have this particularity, each and every one, from the meanest alley sneaker to the proudest, whitest she that ever graced a pontiff's pillow – we have our smiles, as it were, painted on. Those small, cool, quiet Mona Lisa smiles that smile we must, no matter whether it's been fun or it's been not. So all cats have a politician's air; we smile and smile and so they think we're villains. But, I note, this young man is something of ā smiler hisself.

'A sandwich,' he offers. 'And, perhaps, a snifter of brandy.'

His lodgings are poor, though he's handsome enough and even en déshabillé, nightcap and all, there's a neat, smart, dandified air about him. Here is one who knows what's what, thinks I; a man who keeps up appearances in the bedchamber can never embarrass you out of it. And excellent beef sandwiches; I relish a lean slice of roast beef and early learned a taste for spirits, since I started life as a wine-shop cat, hunting cellar rats for my keep, before the world sharpened my wits enough to let me live by them.

And the upshot of this midnight interview? I'm engaged, on the spot, as Sir's valet: valet de chambre and, from time to time, his body servant, for, when funds are running low, as they must do for every gallant officer when the pickings fall off, he pawns the quilt, doesn't he. Then faithful Puss curls up on his chest to keep him warm at nights.

And if he don't like me to knead his nipples, which, out of the purest affection and the desire – ouch! he says – to test the retractability of my claws, I do in moments of absence of mind, then what other valet could slip into a young girl's sacred privacy and deliver her a billet-doux at the very moment when she's reading her prayerbook with her sainted mother? A task I once or twice perform for him, to his infinite gratitude.

And, as you will hear, brought him at last to the best of fortunes for us all.

So Puss got his post at the same time as his boots and I dare say the Master and I have much in common for he's proud as the devil, touchy as tin-tacks, lecherous as liquorice and, though I say it as loves him, as quick-witted a rascal as ever put on clean linen.

When times were hard, I'd pilfer the market for breakfast – a herring, an orange, a loaf; we never went hungry. Puss served him well in the gaming salons, too, for a cat may move from lap to lap with impunity and cast his eye over any hand of cards. A cat can jump on the dice – he can't resist to see it roll! poor thing, mistook it for a bird; and, after I've been, limp-spined, stiff-legged, playing the silly buggers, scooped up to be chastised, who can remember how the dice fell in the first place?

And we had, besides, less ... gentlemanly means of maintenance when they closed the tables to us, as, churlishly, they sometimes did. I'd perform my little Spanish dance while he went round with his hat: *olé!* But he only put my loyalty and affection to the test of this humiliation when the cupboard was as bare as his backside; after, in fact, he'd sunk so low as to pawn his drawers.

So all went right as ninepence and you never saw such boon companions as Puss and his master; until the man must needs go fall in love.

'Head over heels, Puss.'

I went about my ablutions, tonguing my arsehole with the impeccable hygienic integrity of cats, one leg stuck in the air like a ham bone; I choose to remain silent. Love? What has my rakish master, for whom I've jumped through the window of every brothel in the city, besides haunting the virginal back garden of the convent and god knows what other goatish errands, to do with the tender passion?

'And she. A princess in a tower. Remote and shining as Aldebaran. Chained to a dolt and dragon-guarded.'

I withdrew my head from my privates and fixed him with my most satiric smile; I dare him warble on in *that* strain.

'All cats are cynics,' he opines, quailing beneath my yellow glare.

It is the hazard of it draws him, see.

There is a lady sits in a window for one hour and one hour only, at the tenderest time of dusk. You can scarcely see her features, the curtains almost hide her; shrouded like a holy image, she looks out at the piazza as the shops shut up, the stalls go down, the night comes on. And that is all the world she ever sees. Never a girl in all Bergamo so secluded except, on Sundays, they let her go to Mass, bundled up in black, with a veil on. And then she is in the company of an aged hag, her keeper, who grumps along grim as a prison dinner.

How did he see that secret face? Who else but Puss revealed it?

Back we come from the tables so late, so very late at night we found, to our emergent surprise, that all at once it was early in the morning. His pockets were heavy with silver and both our guts sweetly a-gurgle with champagne; Lady Luck had sat with us, what fine spirits were we in! Winter and cold weather. The pious trot to church already with little lanterns through the chill fog as we go ungodly rolling home.

See, a black barque, like a state funeral; and Puss takes it into his bubbly-addled brain to board her. Tacking obliquely to her side, I rub my marmalade pate against her shin; how could any duenna, be she never so stern, take offence at such attentions to her chargeling from a little cat? (As it turns out, this one: *attishooo!* does.) A white hand fragrant as Arabia descends from the black cloak and reciprocally rubs behind his ears at just the ecstatic spot. Puss lets rip a roaring purr, rears briefly on his high-heeled boots; jig with joy and pirouette with glee – she laughs to see and draws her veil aside. Puss glimpses high above, as it were, an alabaster lamp lit behind by dawn's first flush: her face.

And she smiling.

For a moment, just that moment, you would have thought it was May morning.

'Come along! Come! Don't dawdle over the nasty beast!' snaps the old hag, with the one tooth in her mouth, and warts; she sneezes.

The veil comes down; so cold it is, and dark, again.

It was not I alone who saw her; with that smile he swears she stole his heart.

Love.

I've sat inscrutably by and washed my face and sparkling dicky with my clever paw while he made the beast with two backs with every harlot in the city, besides a number of good wives, dutiful daughters, rosy country girls come to sell celery and endive on the corner, and the chambermaid who strips the bed, what's more. The Mayor's wife, even, shed her diamond earrings for him and the wife of the notary un-shuffled her petticoats and, if I could, I would blush to remember how her daughter shook out her flaxen plaits and jumped in bed between them and she not sixteen years old. But never the word, 'love', has fallen from his lips, nor in nor out of any of these transports, until my master saw the wife of Signor Panteleone as she went walking out to Mass, and she lifted up her veil though not for him.

And now he is half sick with it and will go to the tables no more for lack of heart and never even pats the bustling rump of the chamber-maid in his new-found, maudlin celibacy, so we get our slops left festering for days and the sheets filthy and the wench goes banging about bad-temperedly with her broom enough to fetch the plaster off the walls.

I'll swear he lives for Sunday morning, though never before was he a religious man. Saturday nights, he bathes himself punctiliously, even, I'm glad to see, washes behind his ears, perfumes himself, presses his uniform so you'd think he had a right to wear it. So much in love he very rarely panders to the pleasures, even of Onan, as he lies tossing on his couch, for he cannot sleep for fear he miss the summoning bell. Then out into the cold morning, harking after that black, vague shape, hapless fisherman for this sealed oyster with such a pearl in it. He creeps behind her across the square; how can so amorous bear to be so inconspicuous? And yet, he must; though, sometimes, the old hag sneezes and says she swears there is a cat about.

He will insinuate himself into the pew behind milady and sometimes contrive to touch the hem of her garment, when they all kneel, and never a thought to his orisons; she is the divinity he's come to worship. Then sits silent, in a dream, till bed-time; what pleasure is his company for me?

He won't eat, either. I brought him a fine pigeon from the inn kitchen, fresh off the spit, parfumé avec tarragon, but he wouldn't touch it so I crunched it up, bones and all. Performing, as ever after meals, my meditative toilette, I pondered, thus: one, he is in a fair way to ruining us both by neglecting his business; two, love is desire sustained by unfulfilment. If I lead him to her bedchamber and there he takes his fill of her lily-white, he'll be right as rain in two shakes and next day tricks as usual.

Then Master and his Puss will soon be solvent once again.

Which, at the moment, very much not, sir.

This Signor Panteleone employs, his only servant but the hag, a kitchen cat, a sleek, spry tabby whom I accost. Grasping the slack of her neck firmly between my teeth, I gave her the customary tribute of a few firm thrusts of my striped loins and, when she got her breath back, she assured me in the friendliest fashion the old man was a fool and a miser who kept herself on short commons for the sake of the mousing and the young lady a soft-hearted creature who smuggled breast of chicken and sometimes, when the hag-dragon-governess napped at midday, snatched this pretty kitty out of the hearth and into her bedroom to play with reels of silk and run after trailed handkerchiefs, when she and she had as much fun together as two Cinderellas at an all-girls' ball.

Poor, lonely lady, married so young to an old dodderer with his bald pate and his goggle eyes and his limp, his avarice, his gore belly, his rheumaticks, and his flag hangs all the time at half-mast indeed; and jealous as he is impotent, tabby declares – he'd put a stop to all the rutting in the world, if he had his way, just to certify his young wife don't get from another what she can't get from him.

'Then shall we hatch a plot to antler him, my precious?'

Nothing loath, she tells me the best time for this accomplishment should be the one day in all the week he forsakes his wife and his counting-house to ride off into the country to extort most grasping rents from starveling tenant farmers. And she's left all alone, then, behind so many bolts and bars you wouldn't believe; all alone – but for the hag!

Aha! This hag turns out to be the biggest snag; an iron-plated, copper-bottomed, sworn man-hater of some sixty bitter winters who – as ill luck would have it – shatters, clatters, erupts into paroxysms of the *sneeze* at the very glimpse of a cat's whisker. No chance of Puss worming his winsome way into *that* one's affections, nor for my tabby, neither! But, oh my dear, I say; see how my ingenuity rises to this challenge . . . So we resume the sweetest part of our conversation in the dusty convenience of the coalhole and she promises me, least she can do, to see the fair, hitherto-inaccessible one gets a letter safe if I slip it to her and slip it to her forthwith I do, though somewhat discommoded by my boots.

He spent three hours over his letter, did my master, as long as it takes me to lick the coaldust off my dicky. He tears up half a quire of paper, splays five pen-nibs with the force of his adoration: 'Look not for any peace, my heart; having become a slave to this beauty's tyranny, dazzled am I by this sun's rays and my torments cannot be assuaged.' *That's* not the high road to the rumpling of the bedcovers; she's got *one* ninny between them already!

'Speak from the heart,' I finally exhort. 'And all good women have a missionary streak, sir; convince her her orifice will be your salvation and she's yours.'

'When I want your advice, Puss, I'll ask for it,' he says, all at once hoity-toity. But at last he manages to pen ten pages; a rake, a profligate, a card-sharper, a cashiered officer well on the way to rack and ruin when first he saw, as if it were a glimpse of grace, her face . . . his angel, his good angel, who will lead him from perdition.

Oh, what a masterpiece he penned!

'Such tears she wept at his addresses!' says my tabby friend. 'Oh, Tabs, she sobs – for she calls me "Tabs" – I never meant to wreak such havoc with a pure heart when I smiled to see a booted cat! And put his paper next to her heart and swore, it was a good soul that sent her his vows and she was too much in love with virtue to withstand him. If, she adds, for she's a sensible girl, he's neither old as the hills nor ugly as sin, that is.'

An admirable little note the lady's sent him in return, per Figaro here and there; she adopts a responsive yet uncompromising tone. For, says she, how can she usefully discuss his passion further without a glimpse of his person?

He kisses her letter once, twice, a thousand times; she must and will see me! I shall serenade her this very evening!

So, when dusk falls, off we trot to the piazza, he with an old guitar he pawned his sword to buy and most, if I may say so, outlandishly rigged out in some kind of vagabond mountebank's outfit he bartered his gold-braided waistcoat with poor Pierrot braying in the square for, moonstruck zany, lovelorn loon he was himself and even plastered his face with flour to make it white, poor fool, and so ram home his heartsick state.

There she is, the evening star with the clouds around her; but such a creaking of carts in the square, such a clatter and crash as they dismantle the stalls, such an ululation of ballad-singers and oration of nostrum-peddlers and perturbation of errand boys that though he wails out his heart to her: 'Oh, my beloved!', why she, all in a dream, sits with her gaze in the middle distance, where there's a crescent moon stuck on the sky behind the cathedral pretty as a painted stage, and so is she.

Does she hear him?

Not a grace-note.

Does she see him?

Never a glance.

'Up you go, Puss; tell her to look my way!'

If rococo's a piece of cake, that chaste, tasteful, early Palladian stumped many a better cat than I in its time. Agility's not in it, when it comes to Palladian; daring alone will carry the day and, though the first storey's graced with a hefty caryatid whose bulbous loincloth and tremendous pects facilitate the first ascent, the Doric column on her head proves a horse of a different colour, I can tell you. Had I not seen my precious Tabby crouched in the gutter above me keening encouragement, I, even I, might never have braved that flying, upward leap that brought me, as if Harlequin himself on wires, in one bound to her window-sill.

'Dear god!' the lady says, and jumps. I see she, too, ah, sentimental thing! clutches a well-thumbed letter. 'Puss in boots!'

I bow her with a courtly flourish. What luck to hear no sniff or sneeze; where's hag? A sudden flux sped her to the privy – not a moment to lose.

'Cast your eye below,' I hiss. 'Him you know of lurks below, in white with the big hat, ready to sing you an evening ditty.'

The bedroom door creaks open, then, and: whee! through the air Puss goes, discretion is the better part. And, for both their sweet sakes I did it, the sight of both their bright eyes inspired me to the never-before-attempted, by me or any other cat, in boots or out of them – the death-defying triple somersault!

And a three-storey drop to ground, what's more; a grand descent.

Only the merest trifle winded, I'm proud to say, I neatly land on all my fours and Tabs goes wild, huzzah! But has my master witnessed my triumph? Has he, my arse. He's tuning up that old mandolin and breaks, as down I come, again into his song.

I would never have said, in the normal course of things, his voice would charm the birds out of the trees, like mine; and yet the bustle died for him, the homeward-turning costers paused in their tracks to hearken, the preening street girls forgot their hard-edged smiles as they turned to him and some of the old ones wept, they did.

Tabs, up on the roof there, prick up your ears! For by its power I know my heart is in his voice.

And now the lady lowers her eyes to him and smiles, as once she smiled at me.

Then, bang! a stern hand pulls the shutters to. And it was as if all the violets in all the baskets of all the flower-sellers drooped and faded at once; and spring stopped dead in its tracks and might, this time, not come at all; and the bustle and the business of the square, that had so magically quieted for his song, now rose up again with the harsh clamour of the loss of love.

And we trudge drearily off to dirty sheets and a mean supper of bread and cheese, all I can steal him, but at least the poor soul manifests a hearty appetite now she knows he's in the world and not the ugliest of mortals; for the first time since that fateful morning, sleeps sound. But sleep comes hard to Puss tonight. He takes a midnight stroll across the square, soon comfortably discusses a choice morsel of salt cod his tabby friend found among the ashes on the hearth before our converse turns to other matters.

'Rats!' she says. 'And take your boots off, you uncouth bugger; those three-inch heels wreak havoc with the soft flesh of my under-belly!'

When we'd recovered ourselves a little, I ask her what she means by those 'rats' of hers and she proposes her scheme to me. How my master must pose as a *rat-catcher* and I, his ambulant marmalade rat-trap. How we will then go kill the rats that ravage milady's bedchamber, the day the old fool goes to fetch his rents, and she can have her will of the lad at leisure for, if there is one thing the hag fears more than a cat, it is a rat and she'll cower in a cupboard till the last rat is off the premises before she comes out. Oh, this tabby one, sharp as a tack is she! I congratulate her ingenuity with a few affectionate cuffs round the head and home again, for breakfast, ubiquitous Puss, here, there and everywhere, who's your Figaro?

Master applauds the rat ploy; but, as to the rats themselves, how are they to arrive in the house in the first place? he queries.

'Nothing easier, sir; my accomplice, a witty soubrette who lives among the cinders, dedicated as she is to the young lady's happiness, will personally strew a large number of dead and dying rats she has herself collected about the bedroom of the said ingénue's duenna, and, most particularly, that of the said ingénue herself. This to be done tomorrow morning, as soon as Sir Pantaloon rides out to fetch his rents. By good fortune, down in the square, plying for hire, a rat-catcher! Since our hag cannot abide either a rat or a cat, it falls to milady to escort the rat-catcher, none other than yourself, sir, and his intrepid hunter, myself, to the site of the infestation.

'Once you're in her bedroom, sir, if *you* don't know what to do, then I can't help you.'

'Keep your foul thoughts to yourself, Puss.'

Some things, I see, are sacrosanct from humour.

Sure enough, prompt at five in the bleak next morning, I observe with my own eyes the lovely lady's lubbery husband hump off on his horse like a sack of potatoes to rake in his dues. We're ready with our sign: SIGNOR FURIOSO, THE LIVING DEATH OF RATS; and in the leathers he's borrowed from the porter, I hardly recognize him myself, not with the false moustache. He coaxes the chambermaid with a few kisses – poor, deceived girl! love knows no shame – and so we install ourselves under a certain shuttered window with the great pile of traps she's lent us, the sign of our profession, Puss perched atop them bearing the humble yet determined look of a sworn enemy of vermin.

We've not waited more than fifteen minutes – and just as well, so many rat-plagued Bergamots approach us already and are not easily dissuaded from employing us – when the front door flies open on a lusty scream. The hag, aghast, flings her arms round flinching Furioso, how fortuitous to find him! But, at the whiff of me, she's sneezing so valiantly, her eyes awash, the vertical gutters of her nostrils aswill with snot, she barely can depict the scenes inside, rattus domesticus dead in her bed and all; and worse! in the Missus' room.

So Signor Furioso and his questing Puss are ushered into the very sanctuary of the goddess, our presence announced by a fanfare from her keeper on the noseharp. *Attishhoooo ! ! !*

Sweet and pleasant in a morning gown of loose linen, our ingénue jumps at the tattoo of my boot heels but recovers instantly and the wheezing, hawking hag is in no state to sniffle more than: 'Ain't I seen that cat before?'

'Not a chance,' says my master. 'Why, he's come but yesterday with me from Milano.'

So she has to make do with that.

My Tabs has lined the very stairs with rats; she's made a morgue of the hag's room but something more lively of the lady's. For some of her prey she's very cleverly not killed but crippled; a big black beastie weaves its way towards us over the turkey carpet, Puss, pounce! Between screaming and sneezing, the hag's in a fine state, I can tell you, though milady exhibits a most praiseworthy and collected presence of mind, being, I guess, a young woman of no small grasp so, perhaps, she has a sniff of the plot, already.

My master goes down hands and knees under the bed.

'My god!' he cries. 'There's the biggest hole, here in the wainscoting, I ever saw in all my professional career! And there's an army of black rats gathering behind it, ready to storm through! To arms!'

But, for all her terror, the hag's loath to leave the Master and me alone to deal with the rats; she casts her eye on a silver-backed hairbrush, a coral rosary, twitters, hovers, screeches, mutters until milady assures her, amidst scenes of rising pandemonium:

'I shall stay here myself and see that Signor Furioso doesn't make off with my trinkets. You go and recover yourself with an infusion of friar's balsam and don't come back until I call.'

The hag departs; quick as a flash, la belle turns the key in the door on her and softly laughs, the naughty one.

Dusting the slut-fluff from his knees, Signor Furioso now stands slowly upright; swiftly, he removes his false moustache, for no element of the farcical must mar this first, delirious encounter of these lovers, must it. (Poor soul, how his hands tremble!)

Accustomed as I am to the splendid, feline nakedness of my kind, that offers no concealment of that soul made manifest in the flesh of lovers, I am always a little moved by the poignant reticence with which humanity shyly hesitates to divest itself of its clutter of concealing rags in the presence of desire. So, first, these two smile, a little, as if to say: 'How strange to meet you here!', uncertain of a loving welcome, still. And do I deceive myself, or do I see a tear a-twinkle in the corner of his eye? But who is it steps towards the other first? Why, she; women, I think, are, of the two sexes, the more keenly tuned to the sweet music of their bodies. (A penny for my foul thoughts, indeed! Does she, that wise, grave personage in the négligé, think you've staged this grand charade merely in order to kiss her hand?) But, then – oh, what a pretty blush! steps back; now it's his turn to take two steps forward in the saraband of Eros.

I could wish, though, they'd dance a little faster; the hag will soon recover from her spasms and shall she find them in flagrante?

His hand, then, trembling, upon her bosom; hers, initially more hesitant, sequentially more purposeful, upon his breeches. Then their strange trance breaks; that sentimental havering done, I never saw two fall to it with such appetite. As if the whirlwind got into their fingers, they strip each other bare in a twinkling and she falls back on the bed, shows him the target, he displays the dart, scores an instant bullseye. Bravo! Never can that old bed have shook with such a storm before. And their sweet, choked mutterings, poor things: 'I never ...' 'My darling ...' 'More ...' And etc. etc. Enough to melt the thorniest heart.

He rises up on his elbows once and gasps at me: 'Mimic the murder of the rats, Puss! Mask the music of Venus with the clamour of Diana!'

A-hunting we shall go! Loyal to the last, I play catch as catch can with Tab's dead rats, giving the dying the coup de grâce and baying with resonant vigour to drown the extravagant screeches that break forth from that (who would have suspected?) more passionate young woman as she comes off in fine style. (Full marks, Master.)

At that, the old hag comes battering at the door. What's going on? Whyfor the racket? And the door rattles on its hinges.

'Peace!' cries Signor Furioso. 'Haven't I just now blocked the great hole?'

But milady's in no hurry to don her smock again, she takes her lovely time about it; so full of pleasure gratified her languorous limbs you'd think her very navel smiled. She pecks my master prettily thank-you on the cheek, wets the gum on his false moustache with the tip of her strawberry tongue and sticks it back on his upper lip for him, then lets her wardress into the scene of the faux carnage with the most modest and irreproachable air in the world.

'See! Puss has slaughtered all the rats.'

I rush, purring proud, to greet the hag; instantly, her eyes o'erflow.

'Why the bedclothes so disordered?' she squeaks, not quite blinded, yet, by phlegm and chosen for her post from all the other applicants on account of her suspicious mind, even (oh, dutiful) when in grande peur des rats.

'Puss had a mighty battle with the biggest beast you ever saw upon this very bed; can't you see the bloodstains on the sheets? And now, what do we owe you, Signor Furioso, for this singular service?'

'A hundred ducats,' says I, quick as a flash, for I know my master, left to himself, would, like an honourable fool, take nothing.

'That's the entire household expenses for a month!' wails avarice's well-chosen accomplice.

'And worth every penny! For those rats would have eaten us out of house and home.' I see the glimmerings of sturdy backbone in this little lady. 'Go, pay them from your private savings that I know of, that you've skimmed off the housekeeping.'

Muttering and moaning but nothing for it except do as she is bid; and the furious Sir and I take off a laundry basket full of dead rats as souvenir – we drop it, plop! in the nearest sewer. And sit down to one dinner honestly paid for, for a wonder.

But the young fool is off his feed, again. Pushes his plate aside, laughs, weeps, buries his head in his hands and, time and time again, goes to the window to stare at the shutters behind which his sweetheart scrubs the blood away and my dear Tabs rests from her supreme exertions. He sits, for a while, and scribbles; rips the page in four, hurls it aside. I spear a falling fragment with a claw. Dear God, he's took to writing poetry.

'I must and will have her for ever,' he exclaims.

I see my plan has come to nothing. Satisfaction has not satisfied him; that soul they both saw in one another's bodies has such insatiable hunger no single meal could ever appease it. I fall to the toilette of my hinder parts, my favourite stance when contemplating the ways of the world.

'How can I live without her?'

You did so for twenty-seven years, sir, and never missed her for a moment.

'I'm burning with the fever of love!'

Then we're spared the expense of fires.

'I shall steal her away from her husband to live with me.'

'What do you propose to live on, sir?'

'Kisses,' he said distractedly. 'Embraces.'

'Well, you won't grow fat on that, sir; though *she* will. And then, more mouths to feed.'

'I'm sick and tired of your foul-mouthed barbs, Puss,' he snaps. And yet my heart is moved, for now he speaks the plain, clear, foolish rhetoric of love and who is there cunning enough to help him to happiness but I? Scheme, loyal Puss, scheme!

My wash completed, I step out across the square to visit that charming she who's wormed her way directly into my own hitherto-untrammelled heart with her sharp wits and her pretty ways. She exhibits warm emotion to see me; and, oh! what news she has to tell me! News of a rapt and personal nature, that turns my mind to thoughts of the future, and, yes, domestic plans of most familial nature. She's saved me a pig's trotter, a whole, entire pig's trotter the Missus smuggled to her with a wink. A feast! Masticating, I muse.

'Recapitulate,' I suggest, 'the daily motions of Sir Pantaloon when he's at home.'

They set the cathedral clock by him, so rigid and so regular his habits. Up at the crack, he meagrely breakfasts off yesterday's crusts and a cup of cold water, to spare the expense of heating it up. Down to his counting-house, counting out his money, until a bowl of well-watered gruel at midday. The afternoon he devotes to usury, bankrupting, here, a small tradesman, there, a weeping widow, for fun and profit. Dinner's luxurious, at four; soup, with a bit of rancid beef or a tough bird in it – he's an arrangement with the butcher, takes unsold stock off his hands in return for a shut mouth about a pie that had a finger in it. From four-thirty until five-thirty, he unlocks the shutters and lets his wife look out, oh, don't I know! while hag sits beside her to make sure she doesn't smile. (Oh, that blessed flux, those precious loose minutes that set the game in motion!)

And while she breathes the air of evening, why, he checks up on his chest of gems, his bales of silk, all those treasures he loves too much to share with daylight and if he wastes a candle when he so indulges himself, why, any man is entitled to one little extravagance. Another draught of Adam's ale healthfully concludes the day; up he tucks besides Missus and, since she is his prize possession, consents to finger her a little. He palpitates her hide and slaps her flanks: 'What a good bargain!' Alack, can do no more, not wishing to profligate his natural essence. And so drifts off to sinless slumber amid the prospects of tomorrow's gold.

'How rich is he?'

'Croesus.'

'Enough to keep two loving couples?'

'Sumptuous.'

Early in the uncandled morning, groping to the privy bleared with sleep, were the old man to place his foot upon the subfusc yet volatile fur of a shadow-camouflaged young tabby cat –

'You read my thoughts, my love.'

I say to my master: 'Now, you get yourself a doctor's gown, impedimenta all complete or I'm done with you.'

'What's this, Puss?'

'Do as I say and never mind the reason! The less you know of why, the better.'

So he expends a few of the hag's ducats on a black gown with a white collar and his skull cap and his black bag and, under my direction, makes himself another sign that announces, with all due pomposity, how he is Il Famed Dottore: *Aches cured, pains prevented, bones set, graduate of Bologna, physician extraordinary.* He demands to know, is she to play the invalid to give him further access to her bedroom?

'I'll clasp her in my arms and jump out of the window; we too shall both perform the triple somersault of love.'

'You just mind your own business, sir, and let me mind it for you after my own fashion.'

Another raw and misty morning! Here in the hills, will the weather ever change? So bleak it is, and dreary; but there he stands, grave as a sermon in his black gown and half the market people come with coughs and boils and broken heads and I dispense the plasters and the vials of coloured water I'd forethoughtfully stowed in his bag, he too agitato to sell for himself. (And, who knows, might we not have stumbled on a profitable profession for future pursuit, if my present plans miscarry?)

Until dawn shoots his little yet how flaming arrow past the cathedral on which the clock strikes six. At the last stroke, that famous door flies open once again and – *eeeeeeeeeeeech!* the hag lets rip.

'Oh, Doctor, oh, Doctor, come quick as you can; our good man's taken a sorry tumble!'

And weeping fit to float a smack, she is, so doesn't see the doctor's apprentice is most colourfully and completely furred and whiskered.

The old booby's flat out at the foot of the stair, his head at an acute angle that might turn chronic and a big bunch of keys, still, gripped in his right hand as if they were the keys to heaven marked: *Wanted on voyage*. And Missus, in her wrap, bends over him with a pretty air of concern.

'A fall –' she begins when she sees the doctor but stops short when she sees your servant, Puss, looking as suitably down-in-the-mouth as his chronic smile will let him, humping his master's stock-in-trade and hawing like a sawbones. 'You, again,' she says, and can't forbear to giggle. But the dragon's too blubbered to hear.

My master puts his ear to the old man's chest and shakes his head dolefully; then takes the mirror from his pocket and puts it to the old man's mouth. Not a breath clouds it. Oh, sad! Oh, sorrowful!

'Dead, is he?' sobs the hag. 'Broke his neck, has he?'

And she slyly makes a little grab for the keys, in spite of her well-orchestrated distress; but Missus slaps her hand and she gives over.

'Let's get him to a softer bed,' says Master.

He ups the corpse, carries it aloft to the room we know full well, bumps Pantaloon down, twitches an eyelid, taps a kneecap, feels a pulse.

'Dead as a doornail,' he pronounces. 'It's not a doctor you want, it's an undertaker.'

Missus has a handkerchief very dutifully and correctly to her eyes.

'You just run along and get one,' she says to hag. 'And then I'll read the will. Because don't think he's forgotten you, thou faithful servant. Oh, my goodness, no.'

So off goes hag; you never saw a woman of her accumulated Christmases sprint so fast. As soon as they are left alone, no trifling, this time; they're at it, hammer and tongs, down on the carpet since the bed is occupé. Up and down, up and down his arse; in and out, in and out her legs. Then she heaves him up and throws him on his back, her turn at the grind, now, and you'd think she'll never stop.

Toujours discret, Puss occupies himself in unfastening the shutters and throwing the windows open to the beautiful beginnings of morning in whose lively yet fragrant air his sensitive nostrils catch the first and vernal hint of spring. In a few moments, my dear friend joins me. I notice already – or is it only my fond imagination? – a charming new *portliness* in her gait, hitherto so elastic, so spring-heeled. And there we sit upon the window-sill, like the two genii and protectors of the house; ah, Puss, your rambling days are over. I shall become a hearthrug cat, a fat and cosy cushion cat, sing to the moon no more, settle at last amid the sedentary joys of a domesticity we two, she and I, have so richly earned.

Their cries of rapture rouse me from this pleasant revery.

The hag chooses, naturellement, this tender if outrageous moment to return with the undertaker in his chiffoned topper, plus a brace of mutes black as beetles, glum as bailiffs, bearing the elm box between them to take the corpse away in. But they cheer up something wonderful at the unexpected spectacle before them and he and she conclude their amorous interlude amidst roars of approbation and torrents of applause.

But what a racket the hag makes! Police, murder, thieves! Until the Master chucks her purseful of gold back again, for a gratuity. (Meanwhile, I note that sensible young woman, mother-naked as she is, has yet the presence of mind to catch hold of her husband's keyring and sharply tug it from his sere, cold grip. Once she's got the keys secure, she's in charge of all.)

'Now, no more of your nonsense!' she snaps to hag. 'If I hereby give you the sack, you'll get a handsome gift to go along with you for now' – flourishing the keys – 'I am a rich widow and here' – indicating to all my bare yet blissful master – 'is the young man who'll be my second husband.'

When the governess found Signor Panteleone had indeed remembered her in his will, left her a keepsake of the cup he drank his morning water from, she made not a squeak more, pocketed a fat sum with thanks and, sneezing, took herself off with no more cries of 'murder', neither. The old buffoon briskly bundled in his coffin and buried; Master comes into a great fortune and Missus rounding out already and they as happy as pigs in plunk.

But my Tabs beat her to it, since cats don't take much time about engendering; three fine, new-minted ginger kittens, all complete with snowy socks and shirtfronts, tumble in the cream and tangle Missus's knitting and put a smile on every face, not just their mother's and proud father's for Tabs and I smile all day long and, these days, we put our hearts in it.

So may all your wives, if you need them, be rich and pretty; and all your husbands, if you want them, be young and virile; and all your cats as wily, perspicacious and resourceful as:

PUSS-IN-BOOTS.

The Erl-King

The lucidity, the clarity of the light that afternoon was sufficient to itself; perfect transparency must be impenetrable, these vertical bars of a brass-coloured distillation of light coming down from sulphur-yellow interstices in a sky hunkered with grey clouds that bulge with more rain. It struck the wood with nicotine-stained fingers, the leaves glittered. A cold day of late October, when the withered blackberries dangled like their own dour spooks on the discoloured brambles. There were crisp husks of beechmast and cast acorn cups underfoot in the russet slime of dead bracken where the rains of the equinox had so soaked the earth that the cold oozed up through the soles of the shoes, lancinating cold of the approach of winter that grips hold of your belly and squeezes it tight. Now the stark elders have an anorexic look; there is not much in the autumn wood to make you smile but it is not yet, not quite yet, the saddest time of the year. Only, there is a haunting sense of the imminent cessation of being; the year, in turning, turns in on itself. Introspective weather, a sickroom hush.

The woods enclose. You step between the first trees and then you are no longer in the open air; the wood swallows you up. There is no way through the wood any more, this wood has reverted to its original privacy. Once you are inside it, you must stay there until it lets you out again for there is no clue to guide you through in perfect safety; grass grew over the track years ago and now the rabbits and the foxes make their own runs in the subtle labyrinth and nobody comes. The trees stir with a noise like taffeta skirts of women who have lost themselves in the woods and hunt round hopelessly for the way out. Tumbling crows play tig in the branches of the elms they clotted with their nests, now and then raucously cawing. A little stream with soft margins of marsh runs through the wood but it has grown sullen with the time of the year; the silent, blackish water thickens, now, to ice. All will fall still, all lapse.

A young girl would go into the wood as trustingly as Red Riding Hood to her granny's house but this light admits of no ambiguities and, here, she will be trapped in her own illusion because everything in the wood is exactly as it seems.

The woods enclose and then enclose again, like a system of Chinese boxes opening one into another; the intimate perspectives of the wood changed endlessly around the interloper, the imaginary traveller walking towards an invented distance that perpetually receded before me. It is easy to lose yourself in these woods.

The two notes of the song of a bird rose on the still air, as if my girlish and delicious loneliness had been made into a sound. There was a little tangled mist in the thickets, mimicking the tufts of old man's beard that flossed the lower branches of the trees and bushes; heavy bunches of red berries as ripe and delicious as goblin or enchanted fruit hung on the hawthorns but the old grass withers, retreats. One by one, the ferns have curled up their hundred eyes and curled back into the earth. The trees threaded a cat's cradle of half-stripped branches over me so that I felt I was in a house of nets and though the cold wind that always heralds your presence, had I but known it then, blew gentle around me, I thought that nobody was in the wood but me.

Erl-King will do you grievous harm.

Piercingly, now, there came again the call of the bird, as desolate as if it came from the throat of the last bird left alive. That call, with all the melancholy of the failing year in it, went directly to my heart.

I walked through the wood until all its perspectives converged upon a darkening clearing; as soon as I saw them, I knew at once that all its occupants had been waiting for me from the moment I first stepped into the wood, with the endless patience of wild things, who have all the time in the world.

It was a garden where all the flowers were birds and beasts; ash-soft doves, diminutive wrens, freckled thrushes, robins in their tawny bibs, huge, helmeted crows that shone like patent leather, a blackbird with a yellow bill, voles, shrews, fieldfares, little brown bunnies with their ears laid together along their backs like spoons, crouching at his feet. A lean, tall, reddish hare, up on its great hind legs, nose a-twitch. The rusty fox, its muzzle sharpened to a point, laid its head upon his knee. On the trunk of a scarlet rowan a squirrel clung, to watch him; a cock pheasant delicately stretched his shimmering neck from a brake of thorn to peer at him. There was a goat of uncanny whiteness, gleaming like a goat of snow, who turned her mild eyes towards me and bleated softly, so that he knew I had arrived.

He smiles. He lays down his pipe, his elder bird-call. He lays upon me his irrevocable hand.

His eyes are quite green, as if from too much looking at the wood. There are some eyes can eat you.

The Erl-King lives by himself all alone in the heart of the wood in a house which has only the one room. His house is made of sticks and stones and has grown a pelt of yellow lichen. Grass and weeds grow in the mossy roof. He chops fallen branches for his fire and draws his water from the stream in a tin pail.

What does he eat? Why, the bounty of the woodland! Stewed nettles; savoury messes of chickweed sprinkled with nutmeg; he cooks the foliage of shepherd's purse as if it were cabbage. He knows which of the frilled, blotched, rotted fungi are fit to eat; he understands their eldritch ways, how they spring up overnight in lightless places and thrive on dead things. Even the homely wood blewits, that you cook like tripe, with milk and onions, and the egg-yolk yellow chanterelle with its fan-vaulting and faint scent of apricots, all spring up overnight like bubbles of earth, unsustained by nature, existing in a void. And I could believe that it has been the same with him; he came alive from the desire of the woods.

He goes out in the morning to gather his unnatural treasures, he handles them as delicately as he does pigeons' eggs, he lays them in one of the baskets he weaves from osiers. He makes salads of the dandelion that he calls rude names, 'bum-pipes' or 'piss-the-beds', and flavours them with a few leaves of wild strawberry but he will not touch the brambles, he says the Devil spits on them at Michaelmas.

His nanny goat, the colour of whey, gives him her abundant milk and he can make soft cheese that has a unique, rank, amniotic taste. Sometimes he traps a rabbit in a snare of string and makes a soup or stew, seasoned with wild garlic. He knows all about the wood and the creatures in it. He told me about the grass snakes, how the old ones open their mouths wide when they smell danger and the thin little ones disappear down the old ones' throats until the fright is over and out they come again, to run around as usual. He told me how the wise toad who squats among the kingcups by the stream in summer has a very precious jewel in his head. He said the owl was a baker's daughter; then he smiled at me. He showed me how to thread mats from reeds and weave osier twigs into baskets and into the little cages in which he keeps his singing birds.

His kitchen shakes and shivers with birdsong from cage upon cage of singing birds, larks and linnets, which he piles up one on another against the wall, a wall of trapped birds. How cruel it is, to keep wild birds in cages! But he laughs at me when I say that; laughs, and shows his white, pointed teeth with the spittle gleaming on them.

He is an excellent housewife. His rustic home is spick and span. He puts his well-scoured saucepan and skillet neatly on the hearth side by side, like a pair of polished shoes. Over the hearth hang bunches of drying mushrooms, the thin, curling kind they call jew's-ears, which have grown on the elder trees since Judas hanged himself on one; this is the kind of lore he tells me, tempting my half-belief. He hangs up herbs in bunches to dry, too – thyme, marjoram, sage, vervain, southernwood, yarrow. The room is musical and aromatic and there is always a wood fire crackling in the grate, a sweet, acrid smoke, a bright, glancing flame. But you cannot get a tune out of the old fiddle hanging on the wall beside the birds because all its strings are broken.

Now, when I go for walks, sometimes in the mornings when the frost has put its shiny thumbprint on the undergrowth or sometimes, though less frequently, yet more enticingly, in the evenings when the cold darkness settles down, I always go to the Erl-King and he lays me down on his bed of rustling straw where I lie at the mercy of his huge hands.

He is the tender butcher who showed me how the price of flesh is love; skin the rabbit, he says! Off come all my clothes.

When he combs his hair that is the colour of dead leaves, dead leaves fall out of it; they rustle and drift to the ground as though he were a tree and he can stand as still as a tree, when he wants the doves to flutter softly, crooning as they come, down upon his shoulders, those silly, fat, trusting woodies with the pretty wedding rings round their necks. He makes his whistles out of an elder twig and that is what he uses to call the birds out of the air – all the birds come; and the sweetest singers he will keep in cages.

The wind stirs the dark wood; it blows through the bushes. A little of the cold air that blows over graveyards always goes with him, it crisps the hairs on the back of my neck but I am not afraid of him; only, afraid of vertigo, of the vertigo with which he seizes me. Afraid of falling down.

87

Falling as a bird would fall through the air if the Erl-King tied up the winds in his handkerchief and knotted the ends together so they could not get out. Then the moving currents of the air would no longer sustain them and all the birds would fall at the imperative of gravity, as I fall down for him, and I know it is only because he is kind to me that I do not fall still further. The earth with its fragile fleece of last summer's dying leaves and grasses supports me only out of complicity with him, because his flesh is of the same substance as those leaves that are slowly turning into earth.

He could thrust me into the seed-bed of next year's generation and I would have to wait until he whistled me up from my darkness before I could come back again.

Yet, when he shakes out those two clear notes from his bird call, I come, like any other trusting thing that perches on the crook of his wrist.

I found the Erl-King sitting on an ivy-covered stump winding all the birds in the wood to him on a diatonic spool of sound, one rising note, one falling note; such a sweet piercing call that down there came a soft, chirruping jostle of birds. The clearing was cluttered with dead leaves, some the colour of honey, some the colour of cinders, some the colour of earth. He seemed so much the spirit of the place I saw without surprise how the fox laid its muzzle fearlessly upon his knee. The brown light of the end of the day drained into the moist, heavy earth; all silent, all still and the cool smell of night coming. The first drops of rain fell. In the wood, no shelter but his cottage.

That was the way I walked into the bird-haunted solitude of the Erl-King, who keeps his feathered things in little cages he has woven out of osier twigs and there they sit and sing for him.

Goat's milk to drink, from a chipped tin mug; we shall eat the oatcakes he has baked on the hearthstone. Rattle of the rain on the roof. The latch clanks on the door; we are shut up inside with one another, in the brown room crisp with the scent of burning logs that shiver with tiny flame, and I lie down on the Erl-King's creaking palliasse of straw. His skin is the tint and texture of sour cream, he has stiff, russet nipples ripe as berries. Like a tree that bears bloom and fruit on the same bough together, how pleasing, how lovely.

And now – ach! I feel your sharp teeth in the subaqueous depths of your kisses. The equinoctial gales seize the bare elms and make them whizz and whirl like dervishes; you sink your teeth into my throat and make me scream.

The white moon above the clearing coldly illuminates the still tableaux of our embracements. How sweet I roamed, or, rather, used to roam; once I was the perfect child of the meadows of summer, but then the year turned, the light clarified and I saw the gaunt Erl-King, tall as a tree with birds in its branches, and he drew me towards him on his magic lasso of inhuman music.

If I strung that old fiddle with your hair, we could waltz together to the music as the exhausted daylight founders among the trees; we should have better music than the shrill prothalamions of the larks stacked in their pretty cages as the roof creaks with the freight of birds you've lured to it while we engage in your profane mysteries under the leaves.

He strips me to my last nakedness, that underskin of mauve, pearlized satin, like a skinned rabbit; then dresses me again in an embrace so lucid and encompassing it might be made of water. And shakes over me dead leaves as if into the stream I have become.

Sometimes the birds, at random, all singing, strike a chord.

His skin covers me entirely; we are like two halves of a seed, enclosed in the same integument. I should like to grow enormously small, so that you could swallow me, like those queens in fairy tales who conceive when they swallow a grain of corn or a sesame seed. Then I could lodge inside your body and you would bear me.

The candle flutters and goes out. His touch both consoles and devastates me; I feel my heart pulse, then wither, naked as a stone on the roaring mattress while the lovely, moony night slides through the window to dapple the flanks of this innocent who makes cages to keep the sweet birds in. Eat me, drink me; thirsty, cankered, goblin-ridden, I go back and back to him to have his fingers strip the tattered skin away and clothe me in his dress of water, this garment that drenches me, its slithering odour, its capacity for drowning.

Now the crows drop winter from their wings, invoke the harshest season with their cry.

It is growing colder. Scarcely a leaf left on the trees and the birds come to him in even greater numbers because, in this hard weather, it is lean pickings. The blackbirds and thrushes must hunt the snails from hedge bottoms and crack the shells on stones. But the Erl-King gives them corn and when he whistles to them, a moment later you cannot see him for the birds that have covered him like a soft fall of feathered snow. He spreads out a goblin feast of fruit for me, such appalling succulence; I lie above him and see the light from the fire sucked into the black vortex of his eye, the omission of light at the centre, there, that exerts on me such a tremendous pressure, it draws me inwards.

Eyes green as apples. Green as dead sea fruit.

A wind rises; it makes a singular, wild, low, rushing sound.

What big eyes you have. Eyes of an incomparable luminosity, the numinous phosphorescence of the eyes of lycanthropes. The gelid green of your eyes fixes my reflective face. It is a preservative, like a green liquid amber; it catches me. I am afraid I will be trapped in it for ever like the poor little ants and flies that stuck their feet in resin before the sea covered the Baltic. He winds me into the circle of his eye on a reel of birdsong. There is a black hole in the middle of both your eyes; it is their still centre, looking there makes me giddy, as if I might fall into it.

Your green eye is a reducing chamber. If I look into it long enough, I will become as small as my own reflection, I will diminish to a point and vanish. I will be drawn down into that black whirlpool and be consumed by you. I shall become so small you can keep me in one of your osier cages and mock my loss of liberty. I have seen the cage you are weaving for me; it is a very pretty one and I shall sit, hereafter, in my cage among the other singing birds but I – I shall be dumb, from spite.

When I realized what the Erl-King meant to do to me, I was shaken with a terrible fear and I did not know what to do for I loved him with all my heart and yet I had no wish to join the whistling congregation he kept in his cages although he looked after them very affectionately, gave them fresh water every day and fed them well. His embraces were his enticements and yet, oh yet! they were the branches of which the trap itself was woven. But in his innocence he never knew he might be the death of me, although I knew from the first moment I saw him how Erl-King would do me grievous harm.

Although the bow hangs beside the old fiddle on the wall, all the strings are broken so you cannot play it. I don't know what kind of tunes you might play on it, if it were strung again; lullabies for foolish virgins, perhaps, and now I know the birds don't sing, they only cry because they can't find their way out of the wood, have lost their flesh when they were dipped in the corrosive pools of his regard and now must live in cages.

Sometimes he lays his head on my lap and lets me comb his lovely hair for him; his combings are leaves of every tree in the wood and dryly susurrate around my feet. His hair falls down over my knees. Silence like a dream in front of the spitting fire while he lies at my feet and I comb the dead leaves out of his languorous hair. The robin has built his nest in the thatch again, this year; he perches on an unburnt log, cleans his beak, ruffles his plumage. There is a plaintive sweetness in his song and a certain melancholy, because the year is over – the robin, the friend of man, in spite of the wound in his breast from which Erl-King tore out his heart.

Lay your head on my knee so that I can't see the greenish inward-turning suns of your eyes any more.

My hands shake.

I shall take two huge handfuls of his rustling hair as he lies half dreaming, half waking, and wind them into ropes, very softly, so he will not wake up, and, softly, with hands as gentle as rain, I shall strangle him with them.

Then she will open all the cages and let the birds free; they will change back into young girls, every one, each with the crimson imprint of his love-bite on their throats.

She will carve off his great mane with the knife he uses to skin the rabbits; she will string the old fiddle with five single strings of ash-brown hair.

Then it will play discordant music without a hand touching it. The bow will dance over the new strings of its own accord and they will cry out: 'Mother, mother, you have murdered me!'

The Snow Child

Midwinter – invincible, immaculate. The Count and his wife go riding, he on a grey mare and she on a black one, she wrapped in the glittering pelts of black foxes; and she wore high, black, shining boots with scarlet heels, and spurs. Fresh snow fell on snow already fallen; when it ceased, the whole world was white. 'I wish I had a girl as white as snow,' says the Count. They ride on. They come to a hole in the snow; this hole is filled with blood. He says: 'I wish I had a girl as red as blood.' So they ride on again; here is a raven, perched on a bare bough. 'I wish I had a girl as black as that bird's feather.'

As soon as he completed her description, there she stood, beside the road, white skin, red mouth, black hair and stark naked; she was the child of his desire and the Countess hated her. The Count lifted her up and sat her in front of him on his saddle but the Countess had only one thought: how shall I be rid of her?

The Countess dropped her glove in the snow and told the girl to get down to look for it; she meant to gallop off and leave her there but the Count said: 'I'll buy you new gloves.' At that, the furs sprang off the Countess's shoulders and twined round the naked girl. Then the Countess threw her diamond brooch through the ice of a frozen pond: 'Dive in and fetch it for me,' she said; she thought the girl would drown. But the Count said: 'Is she a fish, to swim in such cold weather?' Then her boots leapt off the Countess's feet and on to the girl's legs. Now the Countess was bare as a bone and the girl furred and booted; the Count felt sorry for his wife. They came to a bush of roses, all in flower. 'Pick me one,' said the Countess to the girl. 'I can't deny you that,' said the Count.

So the girl picks a rose; pricks her finger on the thorn; bleeds; screams; falls.

Weeping, the Count got off his horse, unfastened his breeches and thrust his virile member into the dead girl. The Countess reined in her stamping mare and watched him narrowly; he was soon finished.

Then the girl began to melt. Soon there was nothing left of her but a feather a bird might have dropped; a bloodstain, like the trace of a fox's kill on the snow; and the rose she had pulled off the bush. Now the Countess had all her clothes on again. With her long hand, she stroked her furs. The Count picked up the rose, bowed and handed it to his wife; when she touched it, she dropped it.

'It bites!' she said.

The Lady
of the House of Love

At last the revenants became so troublesome the peasants abandoned the village and it fell solely into the possession of subtle and vindictive inhabitants who manifest their presences by shadows that fall almost imperceptibly awry, too many shadows, even at midday, shadows that have no source in anything visible; by the sound, sometimes, of sobbing in a derelict bedroom where a cracked mirror suspended from a wall does not reflect a presence; by a sense of unease that will afflict the traveller unwise enough to pause to drink from the fountain in the square that still gushes spring water from a faucet stuck in a stone lion's mouth. A cat prowls in a weedy garden; he grins and spits, arches his back, bounces away from an intangible on four fear-stiffened legs. Now all shun the village below the château in which the beautiful somnambulist helplessly perpetuates her ancestral crimes.

Wearing an antique bridal gown, the beautiful queen of the vampires sits all alone in her dark, high house under the eyes of the portraits of her demented and atrocious ancestors, each one of whom, through her, projects a baleful posthumous existence; she counts out the Tarot cards, ceaselessly construing a constellation of possibilities as if the random fall of the cards on the red plush tablecloth before her could precipitate her from her chill, shuttered room into a country of perpetual summer and obliterate the perennial sadness of a girl who is both death and the maiden.

Her voice is filled with distant sonorities, like reverberations in a cave: now you are at the place of annihilation, now you are at the place of annihilation. And she is herself a cave full of echoes, she is a system of repetitions, she is a closed circuit. 'Can a bird sing only the song it knows or can it learn a new song?' She draws her long, sharp fingernail across the bars of the cage in which her pet lark sings, striking a plangent twang like that of the plucked heartstrings of a woman of metal. Her hair falls down like tears.

The castle is mostly given over to ghostly occupants but she herself has her own suite of drawing room and bedroom. Closely barred shutters and heavy velvet curtains keep out every leak of natural light. There is a round table on a single leg covered with a red plush cloth on which she lays out her inevitable Tarot; this room is never more than faintly illuminated by a heavily shaded lamp on the mantelpiece and the dark red figured wallpaper is obscurely, distressingly patterned by the rain that drives in through the neglected roof and leaves behind it random areas of staining, ominous marks like those left on the sheets by dead lovers. Depredations of rot and fungus everywhere. The unlit chandelier is so heavy with dust the individual prisms no longer show any shapes; industrious spiders have woven canopies in the corners of this ornate and rotting place, have trapped the porcelain vases on the mantelpiece in soft grey nets. But the mistress of all this disintegration notices nothing.

She sits in a chair covered in moth-ravaged burgundy velvet at the low, round table and distributes the cards; sometimes the lark sings, but more often remains a sullen mound of drab feathers. Sometimes the Countess will wake it for a brief cadenza by strumming the bars of its cage; she likes to hear it announce how it cannot escape.

She rises when the sun sets and goes immediately to her table where she plays her game of patience until she grows hungry, until she becomes ravenous. She is so beautiful she is unnatural; her beauty is an abnormality, a deformity, for none of her features exhibit any of those touching imperfections that reconcile us to the imperfection of the human condition. Her beauty is a symptom of her disorder, of her soullessness.

The white hands of the tenebrous belle deal the hand of destiny. Her fingernails are longer than those of the mandarins of ancient China and each is pared to a fine point. These and teeth as fine and white as spikes of spun sugar are the visible signs of the destiny she wistfully attempts to evade via the arcana; her claws and teeth have been sharpened on centuries of corpses, she is the last bud of the poison tree that sprang from the loins of Vlad the Impaler who picnicked on corpses in the forests of Transylvania.

The walls of her bedroom are hung with black satin, embroidered with tears of pearl. At the room's four corners are funerary urns and bowls which emit slumbrous, pungent fumes of incense. In the centre is an elaborate catafalque, in ebony, surrounded by long candles in enormous silver candlesticks. In a white lace négligé stained a little with blood, the Countess climbs up on her catafalque at dawn each morning and lies down in an open coffin.

A chignoned priest of the Orthodox faith staked out her wicked father at a Carpathian crossroad before her milk teeth grew. Just as they staked him out, the fatal Count cried: 'Nosferatu is dead; long live Nosferatu!' Now she possesses all the haunted forests and mysterious habitations of his vast domain; she is the hereditary commandant of the army of shadows who camp in the village below her château, who penetrate the woods in the form of owls, bats and foxes, who make the milk curdle and the butter refuse to come, who ride the horses all night on a wild hunt so they are sacks of skin and bone in the morning, who milk the cows dry and, especially, torment pubescent girls with fainting fits, disorders of the blood, diseases of the imagination.

But the Countess herself is indifferent to her own weird authority, as if she were dreaming it. In her dream, she would like to be human; but she does not know if that is possible. The Tarot always shows the same configuration: always she turns up La Papesse, La Mort, La Tour Abolie, wisdom, death, dissolution.

On moonless nights, her keeper lets her out into the garden. This garden, an exceedingly sombre place, bears a strong resemblance to a burial ground and all the roses her dead mother planted have grown up into a huge, spiked wall that incarcerates her in the castle of her inheritance. When the back door opens, the Countess will sniff the air and howl. She drops, now, on all fours. Crouching, quivering, she catches the scent of her prey. Delicious crunch of the fragile bones of rabbits and small, furry things she pursues with fleet, four-footed speed; she will creep home, whimpering, with blood smeared on her cheeks. She pours water from the ewer in her bedroom into the bowl, she washes her face with the wincing, fastidious gestures of a cat.

The voracious margin of huntress's nights in the gloomy garden, crouch and pounce, surrounds her habitual tormented somnambulism, her life or imitation of life. The eyes of this nocturnal creature enlarge and glow. All claws and teeth, she strikes, she gorges; but nothing can console her for the ghastliness of her condition, nothing. She resorts to the magic comfort of the Tarot pack and shuffles the cards, lays them out, reads them, gathers them up with a sigh, shuffles them again, constantly constructing hypotheses about a future which is irreversible.

An old mute looks after her, to make sure she never sees the sun, that all day she stays in her coffin, to keep mirrors and all reflective surfaces away from her – in short, to perform all the functions of the servants of vampires. Everything about this beautiful and ghastly lady is as it should be, queen of night, queen of terror – except her horrible reluctance for the role.

Nevertheless, if an unwise adventurer pauses in the square of the deserted village to refresh himself at the fountain, a crone in a black dress and white apron presently emerges from a house. She will invite you with smiles and gestures; you will follow her. The Countess wants fresh meat. When she was a little girl, she was like a fox and contented herself entirely with baby rabbits that squeaked piteously as she bit into their necks with a nauseated voluptuousness, with voles and field-mice that palpitated for a bare moment between her embroidress's fingers. But now she is a woman, she must have men. If you stop too long beside the giggling fountain, you will be led by the hand to the Countess's larder.

All day, she lies in her coffin in her négligé of blood-stained lace. When the sun drops behind the mountain, she yawns and stirs and puts on the only dress she has, her mother's wedding dress, to sit and read her cards until she grows hungry. She loathes the food she eats; she would have liked to take the rabbits home with her, feed them on lettuce, pet them and make them a nest in her red-and-black chinoiserie escritoire, but hunger always overcomes her. She sinks her teeth into the neck where an artery throbs with fear; she will drop the deflated skin from which she has extracted all the nourishment with a small cry of both pain and disgust. And it is the same with the shepherd boys and gipsy lads who, ignorant or foolhardy, come to wash the dust from their feet in the water of the fountain; the Countess's governess brings them into the drawing room where the cards on the table always show the Grim Reaper. The Countess herself will serve them coffee in tiny cracked, precious cups, and little sugar cakes. The hobbledehoys sit with a spilling cup in one hand and a biscuit in the other, gaping at the Countess in her satin finery as she pours from a silver pot and chatters distractedly to put them at their fatal ease. A certain desolate stillness of her eyes indicates she is inconsolable. She would like to caress their lean brown cheeks and stroke their ragged hair. When she takes them by the hand and leads them to her bedroom, they can scarcely believe their luck.

Afterwards, her governess will tidy the remains into a neat pile and wrap it in its own discarded clothes. This mortal parcel she then discreetly buries in the garden. The blood on the Countess's cheeks will be mixed with tears; her keeper probes her fingernails for her with a little silver toothpick, to get rid of the fragments of skin and bone that have lodged there

> Fee fie fo fum
> I smell the blood of an Englishman.

One hot, ripe summer in the pubescent years of the present century, a young officer in the British army, blond, blue-eyed, heavy-muscled, visiting friends in Vienna, decided to spend the remainder of his furlough exploring the little-known uplands of Romania. When he quixotically decided to travel the rutted cart-tracks by bicycle, he saw all the humour of it: 'on two wheels in the land of the vampires'. So, laughing, he sets out on his adventure.

He has the special quality of virginity, most and least ambiguous of states: ignorance, yet at the same time, power in potentia, and, furthermore, unknowingness, which is not the same as ignorance. He is more than he knows – and has about him, besides, the special glamour of that generation for whom history has already prepared a special, exemplary fate in the trenches of France. This being, rooted in change and time, is about to collide with the timeless Gothic eternity of the vampires, for whom all is as it has always been and will be, whose cards always fall in the same pattern.

Although so young, he is also rational. He has chosen the most rational mode of transport in the world for his trip round the Carpathians. To ride a bicycle is in itself some protection against superstitious fears, since the bicycle is the product of pure reason applied to motion. Geometry at the service of man! Give me two spheres and a straight line and I will show you how far I can take them. Voltaire himself might have invented the bicycle, since it contributes so much to man's welfare and nothing at all to his bane. Beneficial to the health, it emits no harmful fumes and permits only the most decorous speeds. How can a bicycle ever be an implement of harm?

A single kiss woke up the Sleeping Beauty in the Wood.

The waxen fingers of the Countess, fingers of a holy image, turn up the card called Les Amoureux. Never, never before . . . never before has the Countess cast herself a fate involving love. She shakes, she trembles, her great eyes close beneath her finely veined, nervously fluttering eyelids; the lovely cartomancer has, this time, the first time, dealt herself a hand of love and death.

> Be he alive or be he dead
> I'll grind his bones to make my bread.

At the mauvish beginnings of evening, the English m'sieu toils up the hill to the village he glimpsed from a great way off; he must dismount and push his bicycle before him, the path too steep to ride. He hopes to find a friendly inn to rest the night; he's hot, hungry, thirsty, weary, dusty . . . At first, such disappointment, to discover the roofs of all the cottages caved in and tall weeds thrusting through the piles of fallen tiles, shutters hanging disconsolately from their hinges, an entirely uninhabited place. And the rank vegetation whispers, as if foul secrets, here, where, if one were sufficiently imaginative, one could almost imagine twisted faces appearing momentarily beneath the crumbling eaves ... but the adventure of it all, and the consolation of the poignant brightness of the hollyhocks still bravely blooming in the shaggy gardens, and the beauty of the flaming sunset, all these considerations soon overcame his disappointment, even assuaged the faint unease he'd felt. And the fountain where the village women used to wash their clothes still gushed out bright, clear water; he gratefully washed his feet and hands, applied his mouth to the faucet, then let the icy stream run over his face.

When he raised his dripping, gratified head from the lion's mouth, he saw, silently arrived beside him in the square, an old woman who smiled eagerly, almost conciliatorily at him. She wore a black dress and a white apron, with a housekeeper's key ring at the waist; her grey hair was neatly coiled in a chignon beneath the white linen headdress worn by elderly women of that region. She bobbed a curtsy at the young man and beckoned him to follow her. When he hesitated, she pointed towards the great bulk of the mansion above them, whose façade loured over the village, rubbed her stomach, pointed to her mouth, rubbed her stomach again, clearly miming an invitation to supper. Then she beckoned him again, this time turning determinedly upon her heel as though she would brook no opposition.

A great, intoxicated surge of the heavy scent of red roses blew into his face as soon as they left the village, inducing a sensuous vertigo; a blast of rich, faintly corrupt sweetness strong enough almost, to fell him. Too many roses. Too many roses bloomed on enormous thickets that lined the path, thickets bristling with thorns, and the flowers themselves were almost too luxuriant, their huge congregations of plush petals somehow obscene in their excess, their whorled, tightly budded cores outrageous in their implications. The mansion emerged grudgingly out of this jungle.

In the subtle and haunting light of the setting sun, that golden light rich with nostalgia for the day that is just past, the sombre visage of the place, part manor house, part fortified farmhouse, immense, rambling, a dilapidated eagle's nest atop the crag down which its attendant village meandered, reminded him of childhood tales on winter evenings, when he and his brothers and sisters scared themselves half out of their wits with ghost stories set in just such places and then had to have candles to light them up newly terrifying stairs to bed. He could almost have regretted accepting the crone's unspoken invitation; but now, standing before the door of time-eroded oak while she selected a huge iron key from the clanking ringful at her waist, he knew it was too late to turn back and brusquely reminded himself he was no child, now, to be frightened of his own fancies.

The old lady unlocked the door, which swung back on melo-dramatically creaking hinges, and fussily took charge of his bicycle, in spite of his protests. He felt a certain involuntary sinking of the heart to see his beautiful two-wheeled symbol of rationality vanish into the dark entrails of the mansion, to, no doubt, some damp outhouse where they would not oil it or check its tyres. But, in for a penny, in for a pound – in his youth and strength and blond beauty, in the invisible, even unacknowledged pentacle of his virginity, the young man stepped over the threshold of Nosferatu's castle and did not shiver in the blast of cold air, as from the mouth of a grave, that emanated from the lightless, cavernous interior.

The crone took him to a little chamber where there was a black oak table spread with a clean white cloth and this cloth was carefully laid with heavy silverware, a little tarnished, as if someone with foul breath had breathed on it, but laid with one place only. Curiouser and curiouser; invited to the castle for dinner, now he must dine alone. All the same, he sat down as she had bid him. Although it was not yet dark outside, the curtains were closely drawn and only the sparing light trickling from a single oil lamp showed him how dismal his surround-ings were. The crone bustled about to get him a bottle of wine and a glass from an ancient cabinet of wormy oak; while he bemusedly drank his wine, she disappeared but soon returned bearing a steaming platter of the local spiced meat stew with dumplings, and a shank of black bread. He was hungry after his long day's ride, he ate heartily and polished his plate with the crust, but this coarse food was hardly the entertainment he'd expected from the gentry and he was puzzled by the assessing glint in the dumb woman's eyes as she watched him eating.

But she darted off to get him a second helping as soon as he'd finished the first one and she seemed so friendly and helpful, besides, that he knew he could count on a bed for the night in the castle, as well as his supper, so he sharply reprimanded himself for his own childish lack of enthusiasm for the eerie silence, the clammy chill of the place.

When he'd put away the second plateful, the old woman came and gestured he should leave the table and follow her once again. She made a pantomime of drinking; he deduced he was now invited to take after-dinner coffee in another room with some more elevated member of the household who had not wished to dine with him but, all the same, wanted to make his acquaintance. An honour, no doubt; in deference to his host's opinion of himself, he straightened his tie, brushed the crumbs from his tweed jacket.

He was surprised to find how ruinous the interior of the house was – cobwebs, worm-eaten beams, crumbling plaster; but the mute crone resolutely wound him on the reel of her lantern down endless corridors, up winding staircases, through the galleries where the painted eyes of family portraits briefly flickered as they passed, eyes that belonged, he noticed, to faces, one and all, of a quite memorable beastliness. At last she paused and, behind the door where they'd halted, he heard a faint, metallic twang as of, perhaps, a chord struck on a harpsichord. And then, wonderfully, the liquid cascade of the song of a lark, bringing to him, in the heart – had he but known it – of Juliet's tomb, all the freshness of morning.

The crone rapped with her knuckles on the panels; the most seductively caressing voice he had ever heard in his life softly called out, in heavily accented French, the adopted language of the Romanian aristocracy: 'Entrez.'

First of all, he saw only a shape, a shape imbued with a faint luminosity since it caught and reflected in its yellowed surfaces what little light there was in the ill-lit room; this shape resolved itself into that of, of all things, a hoop-skirted dress of white satin draped here and there with lace, a dress fifty or sixty years out of fashion but once, obviously, intended for a wedding. And then he saw the girl who wore the dress, a girl with the fragility of the skeleton of a moth, so thin, so frail that her dress seemed to him to hang suspended, as if untenanted in the dank air, a fabulous lending, a self-articulated garment in which she lived like a ghost in a machine. All the light in the room came from a low-burning lamp with a thick greenish shade on a distant mantelpiece; the crone who accompanied him shielded her lantern with her hand, as if to protect her mistress from too suddenly seeing, or their guest from too suddenly seeing her.

So that it was little by little, as his eyes grew accustomed to the half-dark, that he saw how beautiful and how very young the bedizened scarecrow was, and he thought of a child dressing up in her mother's clothes, perhaps a child putting on the clothes of a dead mother in order to bring her, however briefly, to life again.

The Countess stood behind a low table, beside a pretty, silly, gilt-

and-wire birdcage, hands outstretched in a distracted attitude that was almost one of flight; she looked as startled by their entry as if she had not requested it. With her stark white face, her lovely death's head surrounded by long dark hair that fell down as straight as if it were soaking wet, she looked like a shipwrecked bride. Her huge dark eyes almost broke his heart with their waiflike, lost look; yet he was disturbed, almost repelled, by her extraordinarily fleshy mouth, a mouth with wide, full, prominent lips of a vibrant purplish-crimson, a morbid mouth. Even – but he put the thought away from him immediately – a whore's mouth. She shivered all the time, a starveling chill, a malarial agitation of the bones. He thought she must be only sixteen or seventeen years old, no more, with the hectic, unhealthy beauty of a consumptive. She was the châtelaine of all this decay.

With many tender precautions, the crone now raised the light she held to show his hostess her guest's face. At that, the Countess let out a faint, mewing cry and made a blind, appalled gesture with her hands, as if pushing him away, so that she knocked against the table and a butterfly dazzle of painted cards fell to the floor. Her mouth formed a round 'o' of woe, she swayed a little and then sank into her chair, where she lay as if now scarcely capable of moving. A bewildering reception. Tsk'ing under her breath, the crone busily poked about on the table until she found an enormous pair of dark green glasses, such as blind beggars wear, and perched them on the Countess's nose.

He went forward to pick up her cards for her from a carpet that, he saw to his surprise, was part rotted away, partly encroached upon by all kinds of virulent-looking fungi. He retrieved the cards and shuffled them carelessly together, for they meant nothing to him, though they seemed strange playthings for a young girl. What a grisly picture of a capering skeleton! He covered it up with a happier one – of two young lovers, smiling at one another, and put her toys back into a hand so slender you could almost see the frail net of bone beneath the translucent skin, a hand with fingernails as long, as finely pointed, as banjo picks.

At his touch, she seemed to revive a little and almost smiled, raising herself upright.

'Coffee,' she said. 'You must have coffee.' And scooped up her cards into a pile so that the crone could set before her a silver spirit kettle, a silver coffee pot, cream jug, sugar basin, cups ready on a silver tray, a strange touch of elegance, even if discoloured, in this devastated interior whose mistress ethereally shone as if with her own blighted, submarine radiance.

The crone found him a chair and, tittering noiselessly, departed, leaving the room a little darker.

While the young lady attended to the coffee-making, he had time to contemplate with some distaste a further series of family portraits which decorated the stained and peeling walls of the room; these livid faces all seemed contorted with a febrile madness and the blubber lips, the huge, demented eyes that all had in common bore a disquieting resemblance to those of the hapless victim of inbreeding now patiently filtering her fragrant brew, even if some rare grace has so finely transformed those features when it came to her case. The lark, its chorus done, had long ago fallen silent; no sound but the chink of silver on china. Soon, she held out to him a tiny cup of rose-painted china.

'Welcome,' she said in her voice with the rushing sonorities of the ocean in it, a voice that seemed to come elsewhere than from her white, still throat. 'Welcome to my château. I rarely receive visitors and that's a misfortune since nothing animates me half as much as the presence of a stranger ... This place is so lonely, now the village is deserted, and my one companion, alas, she cannot speak. Often I am so silent that I think I, too, will soon forget how to do so and nobody here will ever talk any more.'

She offered him a sugar biscuit from a Limoges plate; her fingernails struck carillons from the antique china. Her voice, issuing from those red lips like the obese roses in her garden, lips that do not move – her voice is curiously disembodied; she is like a doll, he thought, a ventriloquist's doll, or, more, like a great, ingenious piece of clockwork. For she seemed inadequately powered by some slow energy of which she was not in control; as if she had been wound up years ago, when she was born, and now the mechanism was inexorably running down and would leave her lifeless. This idea that she might be an automaton, made of white velvet and black fur, that could not move of its own accord, never quite deserted him; indeed, it deeply moved his heart. The carnival air of her white dress emphasized her unreality, like a sad Columbine who lost her way in the wood a long time ago and never reached the fair.

'And the light. I must apologize for the lack of light ... a hereditary affliction of the eyes ...'

Her blind spectacles gave him his handsome face back to himself twice over; if he presented himself to her naked face, he would dazzle her like the sun she is forbidden to look at because it would shrivel her up at once, poor night bird, poor butcher bird.

Vous serez ma proie.

You have such a fine throat, m'sieu, like a column of marble. When you came through the door retaining about you all the golden light of the summer's day of which I know nothing, nothing, the card called 'Les Amoureux' had just emerged from the tumbling chaos of imagery before me; it seemed to me you had stepped off the card into my darkness and, for a moment, I thought, perhaps, you might irradiate it.

I do not mean to hurt you. I shall wait for you in my bride's dress in the dark.

The bridegroom is come, he will go into the chamber which has been prepared for him.

I am condemned to solitude and dark; I do not mean to hurt you.

I will be very gentle.

(And could love free me from the shadows? Can a bird sing only the song it knows, or can it learn a new song?)

See, how I'm ready for you. I've always been ready for you; I've been waiting for you in my wedding dress, why have you delayed for so long ... it will all be over very quickly.

You will feel no pain, my darling.

She herself is a haunted house. She does not possess herself; her ancestors sometimes come and peer out of the windows of her eyes and that is very frightening. She has the mysterious solitude of ambiguous states; she hovers in a no-man's land between life and death, sleeping and waking, behind the hedge of spiked flowers, Nosferatu's sanguinary rosebud. The beastly forebears on the walls condemn her to a perpetual repetition of their passions.

(One kiss, however, and only one, woke up the Sleeping Beauty in the Wood.)

Nervously, to conceal her inner voices, she keeps up a front of inconsequential chatter in French while her ancestors leer and grimace on the walls; however hard she tries to think of any other, she only knows of one kind of consummation.

He was struck, once again, by the birdlike, predatory claws which tipped her marvellous hands; the sense of strangeness that had been growing on him since he buried his head under the streaming water in the village, since he entered the dark portals of the fatal castle, now fully overcame him. Had he been a cat, he would have bounced backwards from her hands on four fear-stiffened legs, but he is not a cat: he is a hero.

A fundamental disbelief in what he sees before him sustains him, even in the boudoir of Countess Nosferatu herself; he would have said, perhaps, that there are some things which, even if they *are* true, we should not believe possible. He might have said: it is folly to believe one's eyes. Not so much that he does not believe in her; he can see her, she is real. If she takes off her dark glasses, from her eyes will stream all the images that populate this vampire-haunted land, but, since he himself is immune to shadow, due to his virginity – he does not yet know what there is to be afraid of – and due to his heroism, which makes him like the sun, he sees before him, first and foremost, an inbred, highly strung girl child, fatherless, motherless, kept in the dark too long and pale as a plant that never sees the light, half-blinded by some hereditary condition of the eyes. And though he feels unease, he cannot feel terror; so he is like the boy in the fairy tale, who does not know how to shudder, and not spooks, ghouls, beasties, the Devil himself and all his retinue could do the trick.

This lack of imagination gives his heroism to the hero.

He will learn to shudder in the trenches. But this girl cannot make him shudder.

Now it is dark. Bats swoop and squeak outside the tightly shuttered windows. The coffee is all drunk, the sugar biscuits eaten. Her chatter comes trickling and diminishing to a stop; she twists her fingers together, picks at the lace of her dress, shifts nervously in her chair. Owls shriek; the impedimenta of her condition squeak and gibber all around us. Now you are at the place of annihilation, now you are at the place of annihilation. She turns her head away from the blue beams of his eyes; she knows no other consummation than the only one she can offer him. She has not eaten for three days. It is dinner-time. It is bed-time.

> Suivez-moi.
> Je vous attendais.
> Vous serez ma proie.

The raven caws on the accursed roof. 'Dinnertime, dinnertime,' clang the portraits on the walls. A ghastly hunger gnaws her entrails; she has waited for him all her life without knowing it.

The handsome bicyclist, scarcely believing his luck, will follow her into her bedroom; the candles around her sacrificial altar burn with a low, clear flame, light catches on the silver tears stitched to the wall. She will assure him, in the very voice of temptation: 'My clothes have but to fall and you will see before you a succession of mysteries.'

She has no mouth with which to kiss, no hands with which to caress, only the fangs and talons of a beast of prey. To touch the mineral sheen of the flesh revealed in the cool candle gleam is to invite her fatal embrace; in her low, sweet voice, she will croon the lullaby of the House of Nosferatu.

Embraces, kisses; your golden head, of a lion, although I have never seen a lion, only imagined one, of the sun, even if I've only seen the picture of the sun on the Tarot card, your golden head of the lover whom I dreamed would one day free me, this head will fall back, its eyes roll upwards in a spasm you will mistake for that of love and not of death. The bridegroom bleeds on my inverted marriage bed. Stark and dead, poor bicyclist; he has paid the price of a night with the Countess and some think it too high a fee while some do not.

Tomorrow, her keeper will bury his bones under her roses. The food her roses feed on gives them their rich colour, their swooning odour, that breathes lasciviously of forbidden pleasures.

Suivez-moi.

'Suivez-moi!'
The handsome bicyclist, fearful for his hostess's health, her sanity, gingerly follows her hysterical imperiousness into the other room; he would like to take her into his arms and protect her from the ancestors who leer down from the walls.

What a macabre bedroom!

His colonel, an old goat with jaded appetites, had given him the visiting card of a brothel in Paris where, the satyr assured him, ten louis would buy just such a lugubrious bedroom, with a naked girl upon a coffin; offstage, the brothel pianist played the *Dies Irae* on a harmonium and, amidst all the perfumes of the embalming parlour, the customer took his necrophiliac pleasure of a pretended corpse. He had good-naturedly refused the old man's offer of such an initiation; how can he now take criminal advantage of the disordered girl with fever-hot, bone-dry, taloned hands and eyes that deny all the erotic promises of her body with their terror, their sadness, their dreadful, balked tenderness?

So delicate and damned, poor thing. Quite damned.

Yet I do believe she scarcely knows what she is doing.

She is shaking as if her limbs were not efficiently joined together, as if she might shake into pieces. She raises her hands to unfasten the neck of her dress and her eyes well with tears, they trickle down beneath the rim of her dark glasses. She can't take off her mother's wedding dress unless she takes off her dark glasses; she has fumbled the ritual, it is no longer inexorable. The mechanism within her fails her, now, when she needs it most. When she takes off the dark glasses, they slip from her fingers and smash to pieces on the tiled floor. There is no room in her drama for improvisation; and this unexpected, mundane noise of breaking glass breaks the wicked spell in the room, entirely. She gapes blindly down at the splinters and ineffectively smears the tears across her face with her fist. What is she to do now?

When she kneels to try to gather the fragments of glass together, a sharp sliver pierces deeply into the pad of her thumb; she cries out, sharp, real. She kneels among the broken glass and watches the bright bead of blood form a drop. She has never seen her own blood before, not her *own* blood. It exercises upon her an awed fascination.

Into this vile and murderous room, the handsome bicyclist brings the innocent remedies of the nursery; in himself, by his presence, he is an exorcism. He gently takes her hand away from her and dabs the blood with his own handkerchief, but still it spurts out. And so he puts his mouth to the wound. He will kiss it better for her, as her mother, had she lived, would have done.

All the silver tears fall from the wall with a flimsy tinkle. Her painted ancestors turn away their eyes and grind their fangs.

How can she bear the pain of becoming human?

The end of exile is the end of being.

He was awakened by larksong. The shutters, the curtains, even the long-sealed windows of the horrid bedroom were all opened up and light and air streamed in; now you could see how tawdry it all was, how thin and cheap the satin, the catafalque not ebony at all but black-painted paper stretched on struts of wood, as in the theatre. The wind had blown droves of petals from the roses outside into the room and this crimson residue swirled fragrantly about the floor. The candles had burnt out and she must have set her pet lark free because it perched on the edge of the silly coffin to sing him its ecstatic morning song. His bones were stiff and aching, he'd slept on the floor with his bundled-up jacket for a pillow, after he'd put her to bed.

But now there was no trace of her to be seen, except, lightly tossed across the crumpled black satin bedcover, a lace négligé lightly soiled with blood, as it might be from a woman's menses, and a rose that must have come from the fierce bushes nodding through the window. The air was heavy with incense and roses and made him cough. The Countess must have got up early to enjoy the sunshine, slipped outside to gather him a rose. He got to his feet, coaxed the lark on to his wrist and took it to the window. At first, it exhibited the reluctance for the sky of a long-caged thing, but, when he tossed it up on to the currents of the air, it spread its wings and was up and away into the clear blue bowl of the heavens; he watched its trajectory with a lift of joy in his heart.

Then he padded into the boudoir, his mind busy with plans. We shall take her to Zurich, to a clinic; she will be treated for nervous hysteria. Then to an eye specialist, for her photophobia, and to a dentist to put her teeth into better shape. Any competent manicurist will deal with her claws. We shall turn her into the lovely girl she is; I shall cure her of all these nightmares.

The heavy curtains are pulled back, to let in brilliant fusillades of early morning light; in the desolation of the boudoir, she sits at her round table in her white dress, with the cards laid out before her. She has dropped off to sleep over the cards of destiny that are so fingered, so soiled, so worn by constant shuffling that you can no longer make the image out on any single one of them.

She is not sleeping.

In death, she looked far older, less beautiful and so, for the first time, fully human.

I will vanish in the morning light; I was only an invention of darkness.

And I leave you as a souvenir the dark, fanged rose I plucked from between my thighs, like a flower laid on a grave. On a grave.

My keeper will attend to everything.

Nosferatu always attends his own obsequies; she will not go to the graveyard unattended. And now the crone materialized, weeping, and roughly gestured him to begone. After a search in some foul-smelling outhouses, he discovered his bicycle and, abandoning his holiday, rode directly to Bucharest where, at the poste restante, he found a telegram summoning him to rejoin his regiment at once. Much later, when he changed back into uniform in his quarters, he discovered he still had the Countess's rose, he must have tucked it into the breast pocket of his cycling jacket after he had found her body. Curiously enough, although he had brought it so far away from Romania, the flower did not seem to be quite dead and, on impulse, because the girl had been so lovely and her death so unexpected and pathetic, he decided to try and resurrect her rose. He filled his tooth glass with water from the carafe on his locker and popped the rose into it, so that its withered head floated on the surface.

When he returned from the mess that evening, the heavy fragrance of Count Nosferatu's roses drifted down the stone corridor of the barracks to greet him, and his spartan quarters brimmed with the reeling odour of a glowing, velvet, monstrous flower whose petals had regained all their former bloom and elasticity, their corrupt, brilliant, baleful splendour.

Next day, his regiment embarked for France.

The Werewolf

It is a northern country; they have cold weather, they have cold hearts.

Cold; tempest; wild beasts in the forest. It is a hard life. Their houses are built of logs, dark and smoky within. There will be a crude icon of the virgin behind a guttering candle, the leg of a pig hung up to cure, a string of drying mushrooms. A bed, a stool, a table. Harsh, brief, poor lives.

To these upland woodsmen, the Devil is as real as you or I. More so; they have not seen us nor even know that we exist, but the Devil they glimpse often in the graveyards, those bleak and touching townships of the dead where the graves are marked with portraits of the deceased in the naïf style and there are no flowers to put in front of them, no flowers grow there, so they put out small, votive offerings, little loaves, sometimes a cake that the bears come lumbering from the margins of the forest to snatch away. At midnight, especially on Walpurgisnacht, the Devil holds picnics in the graveyards and invites the witches; then they dig up fresh corpses, and eat them. Anyone will tell you that.

Wreaths of garlic on the doors keep out the vampires. A blue-eyed child born feet first on the night of St John's Eve will have second sight. When they discover a witch – some old woman whose cheeses ripen when her neighbours' do not, another old woman whose black cat, oh, sinister! *follows her about all the time*, they strip the crone, search for her marks, for the supernumerary nipple her familiar sucks. They soon find it. Then they stone her to death.

Winter and cold weather.

Go and visit grandmother, who has been sick. Take her the oatcakes I've baked for her on the hearthstone and a little pot of butter.

The good child does as her mother bids – five miles' trudge through the forest; do not leave the path because of the bears, the wild boar, the starving wolves. Here, take your father's hunting knife; you know how to use it.

The child had a scabby coat of sheepskin to keep out the cold, she knew the forest too well to fear it but she must always be on her guard. When she heard that freezing howl of a wolf, she dropped her gifts, seized her knife and turned on the beast.

It was a huge one, with red eyes and running, grizzled chops; any but a mountaineer's child would have died of fright at the sight of it. It went for her throat, as wolves do, but she made a great swipe at it with her father's knife and slashed off its right forepaw.

The wolf let out a gulp, almost a sob, when it saw what had happened to it; wolves are less brave than they seem. It went lolloping off disconsolately between the trees as well as it could on three legs, leaving a trail of blood behind it. The child wiped the blade of her knife clean on her apron, wrapped up the wolf's paw in the cloth in which her mother had packed the oatcakes and went on towards her grandmother's house. Soon it came on to snow so thickly that the path and any footsteps, track or spoor that might have been upon it were obscured.

She found her grandmother was so sick she had taken to her bed and fallen into a fretful sleep, moaning and shaking so that the child guessed she had a fever. She felt the forehead, it burned. She shook out the cloth from her basket, to use it to make the old woman a cold compress, and the wolf's paw fell to the floor.

But it was no longer a wolf's paw. It was a hand, chopped off at the wrist, a hand toughened with work and freckled with old age. There was a wedding ring on the third finger and a wart on the index finger. By the wart, she knew it for her grandmother's hand.

She pulled back the sheet but the old woman woke up, at that, and began to struggle, squawking and shrieking like a thing possessed. But the child was strong, and armed with her father's hunting knife; she managed to hold her grandmother down long enough to see the cause of her fever. There was a bloody stump where her right hand should have been, festering already.

The child crossed herself and cried out so loud the neighbours heard her and come rushing in. They knew the wart on the hand at once for a witch's nipple; they drove the old woman, in her shift as she was, out into the snow with sticks, beating her old carcass as far as the edge of the forest, and pelted her with stones until she fell down dead.

Now the child lived in her grandmother's house; she prospered.

The Company of Wolves

One beast and only one howls in the woods by night.

The wolf is carnivore incarnate and he's as cunning as he is ferocious; once he's had a taste of flesh then nothing else will do.

At night, the eyes of wolves shine like candle flames, yellowish, reddish, but that is because the pupils of their eyes fatten on darkness and catch the light from your lantern to flash it back to you – red for danger; if a wolf's eyes reflect only moonlight, then they gleam a cold and unnatural green, a mineral, a piercing colour. If the benighted traveller spies those luminous, terrible sequins stitched suddenly on the black thickets, then he knows he must run, if fear has not struck him stock-still.

But those eyes are all you will be able to glimpse of the forest assassins as they cluster invisibly round your smell of meat as you go through the wood unwisely late. They will be like shadows, they will be like wraiths, grey members of a congregation of nightmare; hark! his long, wavering howl . . . an aria of fear made audible.

The wolfsong is the sound of the rending you will suffer, in itself a murdering.

It is winter and cold weather. In this region of mountain and forest, there is now nothing for the wolves to eat. Goats and sheep are locked up in the byre, the deer departed for the remaining pasturage on the southern slopes – wolves grow lean and famished. There is so little flesh on them that you could count the starveling ribs through their pelts, if they gave you time before they pounced. Those slavering jaws; the lolling tongue; the rime of saliva on the grizzled chops – of all the teeming perils of the night and the forest, ghosts, hobgoblins, ogres that grill babies upon gridirons, witches that fatten their captives in cages for cannibal tables, the wolf is worst for he cannot listen to reason.

You are always in danger in the forest, where no people are. Step between the portals of the great pines where the shaggy branches tangle about you, trapping the unwary traveller in nets as if the vegetation itself were in a plot with the wolves who live there, as though the wicked trees go fishing on behalf of their friends – step between the gateposts of the forest with the greatest trepidation and infinite precautions, for if you stray from the path for one instant, the wolves will eat you. They are grey as famine, they are as unkind as plague.

The grave-eyed children of the sparse villages always carry knives with them when they go out to tend the little flocks of goats that provide the homesteads with acrid milk and rank, maggoty cheeses. Their knives are half as big as they are, the blades are sharpened daily.

But the wolves have ways of arriving at your own hearthside. We try and try but sometimes we cannot keep them out. There is no winter's night the cottager does not fear to see a lean, grey, famished snout questing under the door, and there was a woman once bitten in her own kitchen as she was straining the macaroni.

Fear and flee the wolf; for, worst of all, the wolf may be more than he seems.

There was a hunter once, near here, that trapped a wolf in a pit. This wolf had massacred the sheep and goats; eaten up a mad old man who used to live by himself in a hut halfway up the mountain and sing to Jesus all day; pounced on a girl looking after the sheep, but she made such a commotion that men came with rifles and scared him away and tried to track him into the forest but he was cunning and easily gave them the slip. So this hunter dug a pit and put a duck in it, for bait, all alive-oh; and he covered the pit with straw smeared with wolf dung. Quack, quack! went the duck and a wolf came slinking out of the forest, a big one, a heavy one, he weighed as much as a grown man and the straw gave way beneath him – into the pit he tumbled. The hunter jumped down after him, slit his throat, cut off all his paws for a trophy.

And then no wolf at all lay in front of the hunter but the bloody trunk of a man, headless, footless, dying, dead.

A witch from up the valley once turned an entire wedding party into wolves because the groom had settled on another girl. She used to order them to visit her, at night, from spite, and they would sit and howl around her cottage for her, serenading her with their misery.

III

Not so very long ago, a young woman in our village married a man who vanished clean away on her wedding night. The bed was made with new sheets and the bride lay down in it; the groom said, he was going out to relieve himself, insisted on it, for the sake of decency, and she drew the coverlet up to her chin and she lay there. And she waited and she waited and then she waited again – surely he's been gone a long time? Until she jumps up in bed and shrieks to hear a howling, coming on the wind from the forest.

That long-drawn, wavering howl has, for all its fearful resonance, some inherent sadness in it, as if the beasts would love to be less beastly if only they knew how and never cease to mourn their own condition. There is a vast melancholy in the canticles of the wolves, melancholy infinite as the forest, endless as these long nights of winter and yet that ghastly sadness, that mourning for their own, irremediable appetites, can never move the heart for not one phrase in it hints at the possibility of redemption; grace could not come to the wolf from its own despair, only through some external mediator, so that, sometimes, the beast will look as if he half welcomes the knife that despatches him.

The young woman's brothers searched the outhouses and the hay-stacks but never found any remains so the sensible girl dried her eyes and found herself another husband not too shy to piss into a pot who spent the nights indoors. She gave him a pair of bonny babies and all went right as a trivet until, one freezing night, the night of the solstice, the hinge of the year when things do not fit together as well as they should, the longest night, her first good man came home again.

A great thump on the door announced him as she was stirring the soup for the father of her children and she knew him the moment she lifted the latch to him although it was years since she'd worn black for him and now he was in rags and his hair hung down his back and never saw a comb, alive with lice.

'Here I am again, missus,' he said. 'Get me my bowl of cabbage and be quick about it.'

Then her second husband came in with wood for the fire and when the first one saw she'd slept with another man and, worse, clapped his red eyes on her little children who'd crept into the kitchen to see what all the din was about, he shouted: 'I wish I were a wolf again, to teach this whore a lesson!' So a wolf he instantly became and tore off the eldest boy's left foot before he was chopped up with the hatchet they used for chopping logs. But when the wolf lay bleeding and gasping its last, the pelt peeled off again and he was just as he had been, years ago, when he ran away from his marriage bed, so that she wept and her second husband beat her.

They say there's an ointment the Devil gives you that turns you into a wolf the minute you rub it on. Or, that he was born feet first and had a wolf for his father and his torso is a man's but his legs and genitals are a wolf's. And he has a wolf's heart.

Seven years is a werewolf's natural span but if you burn his human clothing you condemn him to wolfishness for the rest of his life, so old wives hereabouts think it some protection to throw a hat or an apron at the werewolf, as if clothes made the man. Yet by the eyes, those phosphorescent eyes, you know him in all his shapes; the eyes alone unchanged by metamorphosis.

Before he can become a wolf, the lycanthrope strips stark naked. If you spy a naked man among the pines, you must run as if the Devil were after you.

It is midwinter and the robin, the friend of man, sits on the handle of the gardener's spade and sings. It is the worst time in all the year for wolves but this strong-minded child insists she will go off through the wood. She is quite sure the wild beasts cannot harm her although, well-warned, she lays a carving knife in the basket her mother has packed with cheeses. There is a bottle of harsh liquor distilled from brambles; a batch of flat oatcakes baked on the hearthstone; a pot or two of jam. The flaxen-haired girl will take these delicious gifts to a reclusive grandmother so old the burden of her years is crushing her to death. Granny lives two hours' trudge through the winter woods; the child wraps herself up in her thick shawl, draws it over her head. She steps into her stout wooden shoes; she is dressed and ready and it is Christmas Eve. The malign door of the solstice still swings upon its hinges but she has been too much loved ever to feel scared.

Children do not stay young for long in this savage country. There are no toys for them to play with so they work hard and grow wise but this one, so pretty and the youngest of her family, a little late-comer, had been indulged by her mother and the grandmother who'd knitted her the red shawl that, today, has the ominous if brilliant look of blood on snow. Her breasts have just begun to swell; her hair is like lint, so fair it hardly makes a shadow on her pale forehead; her cheeks are an emblematic scarlet and white and she has just started her woman's bleeding, the clock inside her that will strike, henceforward, once a month.

She stands and moves within the invisible pentacle of her own virginity. She is an unbroken egg; she is a sealed vessel; she has inside her a magic space the entrance to which is shut tight with a plug of membrane; she is a closed system; she does not know how to shiver. She has her knife and she is afraid of nothing.

Her father might forbid her, if he were home, but he is away in the forest, gathering wood, and her mother cannot deny her.

The forest closed upon her like a pair of jaws.

There is always something to look at in the forest, even in the middle of winter – the huddled mounds of birds, succumbed to the lethargy of the season, heaped on the creaking boughs and too forlorn to sing; the bright frills of the winter fungi on the blotched trunks of the trees; the cuneiform slots of rabbits and deer, the herringbone tracks of the birds, a hare as lean as a rasher of bacon streaking across the path where the thin sunlight dapples the russet brakes of last year's bracken.

When she heard the freezing howl of a distant wolf, her practised hand sprang to the handle of knife, but she saw no sign of a wolf at all, nor of a naked man, neither, but then she heard a clattering among the brushwood and there sprang on to the path a fully clothed one, a very handsome young one, in the green coat and wideawake hat of a hunter, laden with carcasses of game birds. She had her hand on her knife at the first rustle of twigs but he laughed with a flash of white teeth when he saw her and made her a comic yet flattering little bow; she'd never seen such a fine fellow before, not among the rustic clowns of her native village. So on they went together, through the thickening light of the afternoon.

Soon they were laughing and joking like old friends. When he offered to carry her basket, she gave it to him although her knife was in it because he told her his rifle would protect them. As the day darkened, it began to snow again; she felt the first flakes settle on her eyelashes but now there was only half a mile to go and there would be a fire, and hot tea, and a welcome, a warm one, surely, for the dashing huntsman as well as for herself.

This young man had a remarkable object in his pocket. It was a compass. She looked at the little round glass face in the palm of his hand and watched the wavering needle with a vague wonder. He assured her this compass had taken him safely through the wood on his hunting trip because the needle always told him with perfect accuracy where the north was. She did not believe it; she knew she should never leave the path on the way through the wood or else she would be lost instantly. He laughed at her again; gleaming trails of spittle clung to his teeth. He said, if he plunged off the path into the forest that surrounded them, he could guarantee to arrive at her grandmother's house a good quarter of an hour before she did, plotting his way through the undergrowth with his compass, while she trudged the long way, along the winding path.

I don't believe you. Besides, aren't you afraid of the wolves?

He only tapped the gleaming butt of his rifle and grinned.

Is it a bet? he asked her. Shall we make a game of it? What will you give me if I get to your grandmother's house before you?

What would you like? she asked disingenuously.

A kiss.

Commonplaces of a rustic seduction; she lowered her eyes and blushed.

He went through the undergrowth and took her basket with him but she forgot to be afraid of the beasts, although now the moon was rising, for she wanted to dawdle on her way to make sure the handsome gentleman would win his wager.

Grandmother's house stood by itself a little way out of the village. The freshly falling snow blew in eddies about the kitchen garden and the young man stepped delicately up the snowy path to the door as if he were reluctant to get his feet wet, swinging his bundle of game and the girl's basket and humming a little tune to himself.

There is a faint trace of blood on his chin; he has been snacking on his catch.

He rapped upon the panels with his knuckles.

Aged and frail, granny is three-quarters succumbed to the mortality the ache in her bones promises her and almost ready to give in entirely. A boy came out from the village to build up her hearth for the night an hour ago and the kitchen crackles with busy firelight. She has her Bible for company, she is a pious old woman. She is propped up on several pillows in the bed set into the wall peasant-fashion, wrapped up in the patchwork quilt she made before she was married, more years ago than she cares to remember. Two china spaniels with liver-coloured blotches on their coats and black noses sit on either side of the fireplace. There is a bright rug of woven rags on the pantiles. The grandfather clock ticks away her eroding time.

We keep the wolves outside by living well.

He rapped upon the panels with his hairy knuckles.

It is your granddaughter, he mimicked in a high soprano.

Lift up the latch and walk in, my darling.

You can tell them by their eyes, eyes of a beast of prey, nocturnal, devastating eyes as red as a wound; you can hurl your Bible at him and your apron after, granny, you thought that was a sure prophylactic against these infernal vermin . . . now call on Christ and his mother and all the angels in heaven to protect you but it won't do you any good.

His feral muzzle is sharp as a knife; he drops his golden burden of gnawed pheasant on the table and puts down your dear girl's basket, too. Oh, my God, what have you done with her?

Off with his disguise, that coat of forest-coloured cloth, the hat with the feather tucked into the ribbon; his matted hair streams down his white shirt and she can see the lice moving in it. The sticks in the hearth shift and hiss; night and the forest has come into the kitchen with darkness tangled in its hair.

He strips off his shirt. His skin is the colour and texture of vellum. A crisp stripe of hair runs down his belly, his nipples are ripe and dark as poison fruit but he's so thin you could count the ribs under his skin if only he gave you the time. He strips off his trousers and she can see how hairy his legs are. His genitals, huge. Ah! huge.

The last thing the old lady saw in all this world was a young man, eyes like cinders, naked as a stone, approaching her bed.

The wolf is carnivore incarnate.

When he had finished with her, he licked his chops and quickly dressed himself again, until he was just as he had been when he came through her door. He burned the inedible hair in the fireplace and wrapped the bones up in a napkin that he hid away under the bed in the wooden chest in which he found a clean pair of sheets. These he carefully put on the bed instead of the tell-tale stained ones he stowed away in the laundry basket. He plumped up the pillows and shook out the patchwork quilt, he picked up the Bible from the floor, closed it and laid it on the table. All was as it had been before except that grandmother was gone. The sticks twitched in the grate, the clock ticked and the young man sat patiently, deceitfully beside the bed in granny's nightcap.

Rat-a-tap-tap.

Who's there, he quavers in granny's antique falsetto.

Only your granddaughter.

So she came in, bringing with her a flurry of snow that melted in tears on the tiles, and perhaps she was a little disappointed to see only her grandmother sitting beside the fire. But then he flung off the blanket and sprang to the door, pressing his back against it so that she could not get out again.

The girl looked round the room and saw there was not even the indentation of a head on the smooth cheek of the pillow and how, for the first time she'd seen it so, the Bible lay closed on the table. The tick of the clock cracked like a whip. She wanted her knife from her basket but she did not dare reach for it because his eyes were fixed upon her – huge eyes that now seemed to shine with a unique, interior light, eyes the size of saucers, saucers full of Greek fire, diabolic phosphorescence.

What big eyes you have.

All the better to see you with.

No trace at all of the old woman except for a tuft of white hair that had caught in the bark of an unburned log. When the girl saw that, she knew she was in danger of death.

Where is my grandmother?

There's nobody here but we two, my darling.

Now a great howling rose up all around them, near, very near, as close as the kitchen garden, the howling of a multitude of wolves; she knew the worst wolves are hairy on the inside and she shivered, in spite of the scarlet shawl she pulled more closely round herself as if it could protect her although it was as red as the blood she must spill.

Who has come to sing us carols, she said.

Those are the voices of my brothers, darling; I love the company of wolves. Look out of the window and you'll see them.

Snow half-caked the lattice and she opened it to look into the garden. It was a white night of moon and snow; the blizzard whirled round the gaunt, grey beasts who squatted on their haunches among the rows of winter cabbage, pointing their sharp snouts to the moon and howling as if their hearts would break. Ten wolves; twenty wolves – so many wolves she could not count them, howling in concert as if demented or deranged. Their eyes reflected the light from the kitchen and shone like a hundred candles.

It is very cold, poor things, she said; no wonder they howl so.

She closed the window on the wolves' threnody and took off her scarlet shawl, the colour of poppies, the colour of sacrifices, the colour of her menses, and, since her fear did her no good, she ceased to be afraid.

What shall I do with my shawl?

Throw it on the fire, dear one. You won't need it again.

She bundled up her shawl and threw it on the blaze, which instantly consumed it. Then she drew her blouse over her head; her small breasts gleamed as if the snow had invaded the room.

What shall I do with my blouse?

Into the fire with it, too, my pet.

The thin muslin went flaring up the chimney like a magic bird and now off came her skirt, her woollen stockings, her shoes, and on to the fire they went, too, and were gone for good. The firelight shone through the edges of her skin; now she was clothed only in her untouched integument of flesh. This dazzling, naked she combed out her hair with her fingers; her hair looked white as the snow outside. Then went directly to the man with red eyes in whose unkempt mane the lice moved; she stood up on tiptoe and unbuttoned the collar of his shirt.

What big arms you have.

All the better to hug you with.

Every wolf in the world now howled a prothalamion outside the window as she freely gave the kiss she owed him.

What big teeth you have!

She saw how his jaw began to slaver and the room was full of the clamour of the forest's Liebestod but the wise child never flinched, even when he answered:

All the better to eat you with.

The girl burst out laughing; she knew she was nobody's meat. She laughed at him full in the face, she ripped off his shirt for him and flung it into the fire, in the fiery wake of her own discarded clothing. The flames danced like dead souls on Walpurgisnacht and the old bones under the bed set up a terrible clattering but she did not pay them any heed.

Carnivore incarnate, only immaculate flesh appeases him.

She will lay his fearful head on her lap and she will pick out the lice from his pelt and perhaps she will put the lice into her mouth and eat them, as he will bid her, as she would do in a savage marriage ceremony.

The blizzard will die down.

The blizzard died down, leaving the mountains as randomly covered with snow as if a blind woman had thrown a sheet over them, the upper branches of the forest pines limed, creaking, swollen with the fall.

Snowlight, moonlight, a confusion of paw-prints.

All silent, all still.

Midnight; and the clock strikes. It is Christmas Day, the were-wolves' birthday, the door of the solstice stands wide open; let them all sink through.

See! sweet and sound she sleeps in granny's bed, between the paws of the tender wolf.

Wolf-Alice

Could this ragged girl with brindled lugs have spoken like we do she would have called herself a wolf, but she cannot speak, although she howls because she is lonely – yet 'howl' is not the right word for it, since she is young enough to make the noise that pups do, bubbling, delicious, like that of a panful of fat on the fire. Sometimes the sharp ears of her foster kindred hear her across the irreparable gulf of absence; they answer her from faraway pine forest and the bald mountain rim. Their counterpoint crosses and criss-crosses the night sky; they are trying to talk to her but they cannot do so because she does not understand their language even if she knows how to use it for she is not a wolf herself, although suckled by wolves.

Her panting tongue hangs out; her red lips are thick and fresh. Her legs are long, lean and muscular. Her elbows, hands and knees are thickly callused because she always runs on all fours. She never walks; she trots or gallops. Her pace is not our pace.

Two-legs looks, four-legs sniffs. Her long nose is always a-quiver, sifting every scent it meets. With this useful tool, she lengthily investigates everything she glimpses. She can net so much more of the world than we can through the fine, hairy, sensitive filters of her nostrils that her poor eyesight does not trouble her. Her nose is sharper by night than our eyes are by day so it is the night she prefers, when the cool reflected light of the moon does not make her eyes smart and draws out the various fragrances from the woodland where she wanders when she can. But the wolves keep well away from the peasants' shotguns, now, and she will no longer find them there.

Wide shoulders, long arms and she sleeps succinctly curled into a ball as if she were cradling her spine in her tail. Nothing about her is human except that she is *not* a wolf; it is as if the fur she thought she wore had melted into her skin and become part of it, although it does not exist. Like the wild beasts, she lives without a future. She inhabits only the present tense, a fugue of the continuous, a world of sensual immediacy as without hope as it is without despair.

When they found her in the wolf's den beside the bullet-riddled corpse of her foster mother, she was no more than a little brown scrap so snarled in her own brown hair they did not, at first, think she was a child but a cub; she snapped at her would-be saviours with her spiky canines until they tied her up by force. She spent her first days amongst us crouched stockstill, staring at the whitewashed wall of her cell in the convent to which they took her. The nuns poured water over her, poked her with sticks to rouse her. Then she might snatch bread from their hands and race with it into a corner to mumble it with her back towards them; it was a great day among the novices when she learned to sit up on her hind legs and beg for a crust.

They found that, if she were treated with a little kindness, she was not intractable. She learned to recognize her own dish; then, to drink from a cup. They found that she could quite easily be taught a few, simple tricks but she did not feel the cold and it took a long time to wheedle a shift over her head to cover up her bold nakedness. Yet she always seemed wild, impatient of restraint, capricious in temper; when the Mother Superior tried to teach her to give thanks for her recovery from the wolves, she arched her back, pawed the floor, retreated to a far corner of the chapel, crouched, trembled, urinated, defecated – reverted entirely, it would seem, to her natural state. Therefore, without a qualm, this nine days' wonder and continuing embarrassment of a child was delivered over to the bereft and un-sanctified household of the Duke.

Deposited at the castle, she huffed and snuffed and smelled only a reek of meat, not the least whiff of sulphur, nor of familiarity. She settled down on her hunkers with that dog's sigh that is only the expulsion of breath and does not mean either relief or resignation.

The Duke is sere as old paper; his dry skin rustles against the bed-sheets as he throws them back to thrust out his thin legs scabbed with old scars where thorns scored his pelt. He lives in a gloomy mansion, all alone but for this child who has as little in common with the rest of us as he does. His bedroom is painted terracotta, rusted with a wash of pain, like the interior of an Iberian butcher's shop, but for himself, nothing can hurt him since he ceased to cast an image in the mirror.

He sleeps in an antlered bed of dull black wrought iron until the moon, the governess of transformations and overseer of somnambulists, pokes an imperative finger through the narrow window and strikes his face: then his eyes start open.

At night, those huge, inconsolable, rapacious eyes of his are eaten up by swollen, gleaming pupil. His eyes see only appetite. These eyes open to devour the world in which he sees, nowhere, a reflection of himself;

he passed through the mirror and now, henceforward, lives as if upon the other side of things.

Spilt, glistering milk of moonlight on the frost-crisped grass; on such a night, in moony, metamorphic weather, they say you might easily find him, if you had been foolish enough to venture out late, scuttling along by the churchyard wall with half a juicy torso slung across his back. The white light scours the fields and scours them again until everything gleams and he will leave paw-prints in the hoar-frost when he runs howling round the graves at night in his lupine fiestas.

By the red early hour of midwinter sunset, all the doors are barred for miles. The cows low fretfully in the byre when he goes by, the whimpering dogs sink their noses in their paws. He carries on his frail shoulders a weird burden of fear; he is cast in the role of the corpse-eater, the body-snatcher who invades the last privacies of the dead. He is white as leprosy, with scrabbling fingernails, and nothing deters him. If you stuff a corpse with garlic, why, he only slavers at the treat: cadavre provençale. He will use the holy cross as a scratching post and crouch above the font to thirstily lap up holy water.

She sleeps in the soft, warm ashes of the hearth; beds are traps, she will not stay in one. She can perform the few, small tasks to which the nuns trained her, she sweeps up the hairs, vertebrae and phalanges that litter his room into a dustpan, she makes up his bed at sunset, when he leaves it and the grey beasts outside howl, as if they know his transformation is their parody. Unkind to their prey, to their own they are tender; had the Duke been a wolf, they would have angrily expelled him from the pack, he would have had to lollop along miles behind them, creeping in submission on his belly up to the kill only after they had eaten and were sleeping, to gnaw the well-chewed bones and chew the hide. Yet, suckled as she was by wolves on the high uplands where her mother bore and left her, only his kitchen maid, who is not wolf or woman, knows no better than to do his chores for him.

She grew up with wild beasts. If you could transport her, in her filth, rags and feral disorder, to the Eden of our first beginnings where Eve and grunting Adam squat on a daisy bank, picking the lice from one another's pelts, then she might prove to be the wise child who leads them all and her silence and her howling a language as authentic as any language of nature. In a world of talking beasts and flowers, she would be the bud of flesh in the kind lion's mouth: but how can the bitten apple flesh out its scar again?

Mutilation is her lot; though, now and then, she will emit an involuntary rustle of sound, as if the unused chords in her throat were a wind-harp that moved with the random impulses of the air, her whisper, more obscure than the voices of the dumb.

Familiar desecrations in the village graveyard. The coffin had been ripped open with the abandon with which a child unwraps a gift on Christmas morning and, of its contents, not a trace could be found but for a rag of the bridal veil in which the corpse had been wrapped that was caught, fluttering, in the brambles at the churchyard gate so they knew which way he had taken it, towards his gloomy castle.

In the lapse of time, the trance of being of that exiled place, this girl grew amongst things she could neither name nor perceive. How did she think, how did she feel, this perennial stranger with her furred thoughts and her primal sentience that existed in a flux of shifting impressions; there are no words to describe the way she negotiated the abyss between her dreams, those wakings strange as her sleepings. The wolves had tended her because they knew she was an imperfect wolf; we secluded her in animal privacy out of fear of her imperfection because it showed us what we might have been, and so time passed, although she scarcely knew it. Then she began to bleed.

Her first blood bewildered her. She did not know what it meant and the first stirrings of surmise that ever she felt were directed towards its possible cause. The moon had been shining into the kitchen when she woke to feel the trickle between her thighs and it seemed to her that a wolf who, perhaps, was fond of her, as wolves were, and who lived, perhaps, in the moon? must have nibbled her cunt while she was sleeping, had subjected her to a series of affectionate nips too gentle to wake her yet sharp enough to break the skin. The shape of this theory was blurred yet, out of it, there took root a kind of wild reasoning, as it might have from a seed dropped in her brain off the foot of a flying bird.

The flow continued for a few days, which seemed to her an endless time. She had, as yet, no direct notion of past, or of future, or of duration, only of a dimensionless, immediate moment. At night, she prowled the empty house looking for rags to sop the blood up; she had learned a little elementary hygiene in the convent, enough to know how to bury her excrement and cleanse herself of her natural juices, although the nuns had not the means to inform her how it should be, it was not fastidiousness but shame that made her do so.

She found towels, sheets and pillowcases in closets that had not been opened since the Duke came shrieking into the world with all his teeth, to bite his mother's nipple off and weep. She found once-worn ball dresses in cobwebbed wardrobes, and, heaped in the corners of his bloody chamber, shrouds, nightdresses and burial clothes that had wrapped items on the Duke's menus. She tore strips of the most absorbent fabrics to clumsily diaper herself. In the course of these prowlings, she bumped against that mirror over whose surface the Duke passed like a wind on ice.

First, she tried to nuzzle her reflection; then, nosing it industriously, she soon realized it gave out no smell. She bruised her muzzle on the cold glass and broke her claws trying to tussle with this stranger. She saw, with irritation, then amusement, how it mimicked every gesture of hers when she raised her forepaw to scratch herself or dragged her bum along the dusty carpet to rid herself of a slight discomfort in her hindquarters. She rubbed her head against her reflected face, to show that she felt friendly towards it, and felt a cool, solid, immovable surface between herself and she – some kind, possibly, of invisible cage? In spite of this barrier, she was lonely enough to ask this creature to try to play with her, baring her teeth and grinning; at once she received a reciprocal invitation. She rejoiced; she began to whirl round on herself, yapping exultantly, but, when she retreated from the mirror, she halted in the midst of her ecstasy, puzzled, to see how her new friend grew less in size.

The moonlight spilled into the Duke's motionless bedroom from behind a cloud and she saw how pale this wolf, not-wolf who played with her was. The moon and mirrors have this much in common: you cannot see behind them. Moonlit and white, Wolf-Alice looked at herself in the mirror and wondered whether there she saw the beast who came to bite her in the night. Then her sensitive ears pricked at the sound of a step in the hall; trotting at once back to her kitchen, she encountered the Duke with the leg of a man over his shoulder. Her toenails clicked against the stairs as she padded incuriously past, she, the serene, inviolable one in her absolute and verminous innocence.

Soon the flow ceased. She forgot it. The moon vanished; but, little by little, reappeared. When it again visited her kitchen at full strength, Wolf-Alice was surprised into bleeding again and so it went on, with a punctuality that transformed her vague grip on time. She learned to expect these bleedings, to prepare her rags against them, and afterwards, neatly to bury the dirtied things. Sequence asserted itself with custom and then she understood the circumambulatory principle of the clock perfectly, even if all clocks were banished from the den where she and the Duke inhabited their separate solitudes, so that you might say she discovered the very action of time by means of this returning cycle.

When she curled up among the cinders, the colour, texture and warmth of them brought her foster mother's belly out of the past and printed it on her flesh; her first conscious memory, painful as the first time the nuns combed her hair. She howled a little, in a firmer, deepening trajectory, to obtain the inscrutable consolation of the wolves' response, for now the world around her was assuming form. She perceived an essential difference between herself and her surroundings that you might say she could not put her *finger* on – only, the trees and grass of the meadows outside no longer seemed the emanation of her questing nose and erect ears, and yet sufficient to itself, but a kind of backdrop for her, that waited for her arrivals to give it meaning. She saw herself upon it and her eyes, with their sombre clarity, took on a veiled, introspective look.

She would spend hours examining the new skin that had been born, it seemed to her, of her bleeding. She would lick her soft upholstery with her long tongue and groom her hair with her fingernails. She examined her new breasts with curiosity; the white growths reminded her of nothing so much as the night-sprung puffballs she had found, sometimes, on evening rambles in the woods, a natural if disconcerting apparition, but then, to her astonishment, she found a little diadem of fresh hairs tufting between her thighs. She showed it to her mirror littermate, who reassured her by showing her she shared it.

The damned Duke haunts the graveyard; he believes himself to be both less and more than a man, as if his obscene difference were a sign of grace. During the day, he sleeps. His mirror faithfully reflects his bed but never the meagre shape within the disordered covers.

Sometimes, on those white nights when she was left alone in the house, she dragged out his grandmother's ball dresses and rolled on suave velvet and abrasive lace because to do so delighted her adolescent skin. Her intimate in the mirror wound the old clothes round herself, wrinkling its nose in delight at the ancient yet still potent scents of musk and civet that woke up in the sleeves and bodices. This habitual, at last boring, fidelity to her every movement finally woke her up to the regretful possibility that her companion was, in fact, no more than a particularly ingenious variety of the shadow she cast on sunlit grass. Had not she and the rest of the litter tussled and romped with their shadows long ago? She poked her agile nose around the back of the mirror; she found only dust, a spider stuck in his web, a heap of rags. A little moisture leaked from the corners of her eyes, yet her relation with the mirror was now far more intimate since she knew she saw herself within it.

She pawed and tumbled the dress the Duke had tucked away behind the mirror for a while. The dust was soon shaken out of it; she experimentally inserted her front legs in the sleeves. Although the dress was torn and crumpled, it was so white and of such a sinuous texture that she thought, before she put it on, she must thoroughly wash off her coat of ashes in the water from the pump in the yard, which she knew how to manipulate with her cunning forepaw. In the mirror, she saw how this white dress made her shine.

Although she could not run so fast on two legs in petticoats, she trotted out in her new dress to investigate the odorous October hedge-rows, like a débutante from the castle, delighted with herself but still, now and then, singing to the wolves with a kind of wistful triumph, because now she knew how to wear clothes and so had put on the visible sign of her difference from them.

Her footprints on damp earth are beautiful and menacing as those Man Friday left.

The young husband of the dead bride spent a long time planning his revenge. He filled the church with an arsenal of bells, books and candles; a battery of silver bullets; they brought a ten-gallon tub of holy water in a wagon from the city, where it had been blessed by the Archbishop himself, to drown the Duke, if the bullets bounced off him. They gathered in the church to chant a litany and wait for the one who would visit with the first deaths of winter.

She goes out at night more often now; the landscape assembles itself about her, she informs it with her presence. She is its significance.

It seemed to her the congregation in the church was ineffectually attempting to imitate the wolves' chorus. She lent them the assistance of her own, educated voice for a while, rocking contemplatively on her haunches by the graveyard gate; then her nostrils twitched to catch the rank stench of the dead that told her her co-habitor was at hand; raising her head, who did her new, keen eyes spy but the lord of cob-web castle intent on performing his cannibal rituals?

And if her nostrils flare suspiciously at the choking reek of incense and his do not, that is because she is far more sentient than he. She will, therefore, run, run! when she hears the crack of bullets, because they killed her foster mother; so, with the self-same lilting lope, drenched with holy water, will he run, too, until the young widower fires the silver bullet that bites his shoulder and drags off half his fictive pelt, so that he must rise up like any common forked biped and limp distressfully on as best he may.

When they saw the white bride leap out of the tombstones and scamper off towards the castle with the werewolf stumbling after, the peasants thought the Duke's dearest victim had come back to take matters into her own hands. They ran screaming from the presence of a ghostly vengeance on him.

Poor, wounded thing . . . locked half and half between such strange states, an aborted transformation, an incomplete mystery, now he lies writhing on his black bed in the room like a Mycenaean tomb, howls like a wolf with his foot in a trap or a woman in labour, and bleeds.

First, she was fearful when she heard the sound of pain, in case it hurt her, as it had done before. She prowled round the bed, growling, snuffing at his wound that does not smell like her wound. Then, she was pitiful as her gaunt grey mother; she leapt upon his bed to lick, without hesitation, without disgust, with a quick, tender gravity, the blood and dirt from his cheeks and forehead.

The lucidity of the moonlight lit the mirror propped against the red wall; the rational glass, the master of the visible, impartially recorded the crooning girl.

As she continued her ministrations, this glass, with infinite slowness, yielded to the reflexive strength of its own material construction. Little by little, there appeared within it, like the image on photographic paper that emerges, first, a formless web of tracery, the prey caught in its own fishing net, then in firmer yet still shadowed outline until at last as vivid as real life itself, as if brought into being by her soft, moist, gentle tongue, finally, the face of the Duke.

READ MORE IN PENGUIN

In every corner of the world, on every subject under the sun, Penguin represents quality and variety – the very best in publishing today.

For complete information about books available from Penguin – including Puffins, Penguin Classics and Arkana – and how to order them, write to us at the appropriate address below. Please note that for copyright reasons the selection of books varies from country to country.

In the United Kingdom: Please write to *Dept. JC, Penguin Books Ltd, FREEPOST, West Drayton, Middlesex UB7 0BR*

If you have any difficulty in obtaining a title, please send your order with the correct money, plus ten per cent for postage and packaging, to *PO Box No. 11, West Drayton, Middlesex UB7 0BR*

In the United States: Please write to *Penguin USA Inc., 375 Hudson Street, New York, NY 10014*

In Canada: Please write to *Penguin Books Canada Ltd, 10 Alcorn Avenue, Suite 300, Toronto, Ontario M4V 3B2*

In Australia: Please write to *Penguin Books Australia Ltd, 487 Maroondah Highway, Ringwood, Victoria 3134*

In New Zealand: Please write to *Penguin Books (NZ) Ltd,182–190 Wairau Road, Private Bag, Takapuna, Auckland 9*

In India: Please write to *Penguin Books India Pvt Ltd, 706 Eros Apartments, 56 Nehru Place, New Delhi 110 019*

In the Netherlands: Please write to *Penguin Books Netherlands B.V., Keizersgracht 231 NL–1016 DV Amsterdam*

In Germany: Please write to *Penguin Books Deutschland GmbH, Friedrichstrasse 10–12, W–6000 Frankfurt/Main 1*

In Spain: Please write to *Penguin Books S. A., C. San Bernardo 117–6° E–28015 Madrid*

In Italy: Please write to *Penguin Italia s.r.l., Via Felice Casati 20, I–20124 Milano*

In France: Please write to *Penguin France S. A., 17 rue Lejeune, F–31000 Toulouse*

In Japan: Please write to *Penguin Books Japan, Ishikiribashi Building, 2–5–4, Suido, Tokyo 112*

In Greece: Please write to *Penguin Hellas Ltd, Dimocritou 3, GR–106 71 Athens*

In South Africa: Please write to *Longman Penguin Southern Africa (Pty) Ltd, Private Bag X08, Bertsham 2013*

BY THE SAME AUTHOR

Heroes and Villains

After the apocalypse the world is neatly divided. Rational civilization rests with the Professors in their steel and concrete villages; marauding tribes of Barbarians roam the surrounding jungles; mutilated Out People inhabit the burnt scars of cities

But Marianne, Professor's daughter, is carried away into the jungle – a grotesque vegetable paradise – where she will become the captive bride of Jewel, the proud and beautiful Barbarian. There she will witness the savage rituals of the snake worshippers, indulge her voluptuous, virginal fantasies, taste the forbidden fruit of chaos . . .

Erotic, exotic and bizarre, *Heroes and Villains* is a post-apocalyptic romance, a gripping adventure story, a colourful embroidery of religion and magic and, not least, a dispassionate vision of life beyond our brave nuclear world.

The Infernal Desire Machines of Doctor Hoffman

The story of a war fought against the diabolic Doctor Hoffman who wanted to demolish the structures of reason and liberate man from the chains of the reality principle for ever.

Doctor Hoffman chose the human mind and the human heart for his battleground – and it was left to Desiderio to stop him.

'Combines exquisite craft with an apparently boundless reach' – Ian McEwan, author of *First Love, Last Rites*